THE DISTANT TIDE

HEARTS OF IRELAND: BOOK 1

HEATHER DAY GILBERT

The Distant Tide

By: Heather Day Gilbert

Second Edition:
Copyright 2020 Heather Day Gilbert

First Edition: Barbour Publishing,
The Message in a Bottle Romance Collection, 2017

Cover Design by Carpe Librum Book Design
Published by WoodHaven Press

All rights reserved. No part of this publication may be reproduced in any form, stored in any retrieval system, posted on any website, or transmitted in any form or by any means, without written permission from the publisher, except for brief quotations in printed reviews and articles.

Series: Gilbert, Heather Day. Hearts of Ireland; 1

Subject: Ireland—fiction; Genre: Romance fiction; Historical fiction; Christian fiction

Author Information & Newsletter: http://www.heatherdaygilbert.com

CHAPTER 1

1170 AD, Ciar's Kingdom, Ireland

The skies were as unsettled as her own future.

Swirling mountain breezes billowed through Britta's narrow castle window, carrying with them the unmistakable tang of a storm. The sunshine of the morning had given way to glowering clouds this evening. Springtime in Ireland could be fickle.

She swiped at another errant tear. Refocusing on her favorite book, her finger traced the Latin words on the ancient vellum page.

A sharp rap sounded, and her nursemaid, Florie, entered her room in her usual way, without waiting for permission. She bustled toward Britta's chair, her brass-blond hair escaping her kerchief. Her round face was flushed from walking up the tight circular stairs.

"I've been shoutin' for you, Princess. There's no one to come and fetch you, since your father took my servants with him on his journey to see the high king. It's time for our evening meal."

Florie was bolder than any other servant in the castle, but

for good reason. After Britta's mother had died young from the fever, Florie had stepped in to care for the toddler princess. Britta couldn't recall one day when her loyal Florie hadn't come rushing when she needed her.

The woman leaned closer, the smell of cooked meat wafting from her clothing. She cupped Britta's quivering chin with her rough hand then pushed black strands of hair off Britta's face. "You've been crying. What worries could be weighing on you, safe and healthy as you are?"

That was just the problem. She was perfectly safe here in the castle—so comfortable, she never had to leave this place. And the largest part of her didn't want to leave. Generations ago, the O'Shea family had settled in this lush pocket of Ireland. This beloved castle and land held her close, as tightly as if she were shackled.

She tried to explain. "You know I've always wanted to share my faith with those who have never heard of Christ, and even to those who still hold to druidry."

Florie nodded, thoughtful. A smile broke across her face. "Perhaps your father will make your dream possible with this journey. You are of marriageable age now, and I have heard the high king has four handsome sons—"

Britta gasped at the suggestion. Surely her father had traveled to discuss kingdom business with the high king, as he did every year. "I can't leave you, Florie. Nor could I leave Father, although he might not miss the opinions I so freely offer him."

"True, I shouldn't like to see you leave, Princess. I doubt your father would, either." Florie's light eyes crinkled. "Perhaps God has another suitor for you, closer to home."

Britta sighed. She didn't want to think about suitors yet. She wanted to understand how to use her talents for God—whatever those talents were. She was a proficient reader. She also enjoyed talking to Father about decisions for the kingdom, but every time she shared her thoughts, it was as though she was talking into the wind. Father listened to his right-hand man, Ronan. Not to her.

The psalmist said she should ask for the desires of her heart, but the two strongest desires were irreconcilable. There was no way to spread the Word without leaving the kingdom she cared so deeply about.

Florie patted her hand. "Come on down to eat. You'll feel better with something in your stomach, and then I can prepare a bath for you." She rustled down the stairs without waiting for Britta's response.

Not even vaguely mollified, Britta glanced out the window. The low gray clouds obscured her view of the nearby mountain. Because its crowning rock formation was shaped like a crow's beak, many viewed the monument as an annoyance, an obstruction to the clean line of rolling green hills that swept to the ocean. But to her, it felt like a protective ally, solid and reliable. Even though it was simply called Crow Mountain, she liked to imagine more poetic names for it, like Eagle Aerie or Piney Bluff.

If only God would make His plans for her as obvious as that mountain.

WHEN BRITTA RELUCTANTLY TRAILED DOWNSTAIRS, she caught Ronan and Florie attempting to move the tabletop onto the trestle in the great hall. To save space, the table was always taken apart after meals and moved into a corner.

The tabletop was a dense plank of cherrywood, and it would be impossible for two people to manage it, even given Ronan's considerable strength. The guards her father had left behind were already camped at their posts for the evening.

"Let me help." She grabbed a beveled corner, ignoring their

black looks. They didn't want the princess to sully her hands with menial labor. But she *was* the princess, wasn't she? Even though Ronan had been left in charge, she could still do as she pleased.

After considerable effort, they successfully maneuvered the tabletop into position. Cringing to think of repeating the task before each meal, Britta declared, "We will leave the tabletop where it is for the duration of my father's absence."

Florie murmured her approval of this plan then scurried off to the kitchen to retrieve the food.

Ronan, too, nodded in agreement. He removed his mace from his belt and propped it against the wall, near his shield and sword.

As always, Britta felt a wave of thanks that her father had left his best warrior behind to protect her. Ronan's family had lived near the castle all her life, and he had battled alongside her father many times. His loyalty was unquestionable.

Glancing at his mace, a shudder passed from head to toe as she imagined the damage the heavy spiked weapon could inflict. A nervous giggle escaped as she tried to picture such a gentle-spirited man wielding such a deadly weapon, although his build was undeniably powerful and she knew he would not hesitate to protect her life with his own.

He glanced up, his dark eyes softening. "Is something amusing?"

Before she could explain, Florie emerged with a large pot of onion soup. She served it up, accompanied by a hunk of white cheese and slightly scorched oatcakes. Finally, she took her seat, waiting for a look from Britta.

Nodding, Britta sipped her soup, the cue that others could eat. She took an oatcake from the pewter dish then cast a furtive look down the table.

Florie started to wipe her mouth on her sleeve then instead used her linen napkin. "Pray tell, what d'you need, Princess?"

"Have you any of the bog butter? I find it gives my oatcakes incomparable flavor."

"I surely do, and I don't know how I forgot to set it out." Florie hastened into the larder, returning with a greeny-black butter ball.

"Thank you. I know Father says it's uncouth, but I've found nothing matches its taste."

As she finished slathering a thick layer of butter on the oatcake, Ronan spoke. "I shall be riding over to Brennan's castle to trade horses in the morning. Would you care to accompany me?"

It seemed a careless question, a discussion to pass the time, until Britta raised her eyes and met Ronan's dark ones. His completely unguarded gaze struck her like the lightning that had finally loosed outside.

She took in his intense look, his half-quirked smile. He was so expectant, so…*fixed* on what she would answer. Realization dawned. Ronan found her desirable. Had her giggling led him to think she was admiring him?

Or had he felt this ardor for some time? If so, how had she missed it?

An embarrassed flush covered her cheeks. She tried to invent an excuse. "My stomach…perhaps I need to…" Unable to continue, she stood and rushed from the great hall. She heard Ronan shove his chair back to stand, and Florie's anxious voice trailed after her, but she could not stop.

Bolting into her room, she threw herself on her bed, thoughts fluttering about like doves' wings.

How long had Ronan found her attractive? For so many years, they had they wandered the land together, discussing everything from hawks to laws to books. Had the storm-charged air, coupled with her father's absence, released his hidden feelings?

A sudden thought wormed its way to the forefront. What if

this unexpected option was the simple solution to her future, a way to ensure that she could stay in her castle for life? Surely her father would be pleased if she married his right-hand man—the one he would doubtless leave his castle to, since he had no male heirs.

This time, no books could assuage the pounding of her heart. Outside, thunder pounded and rain swept across the moors, spraying mist into her open windows. She jumped from her bed, slamming the shutters together and drawing the iron bar across them for good measure. She wished she could lock her thoughts away so easily, but it was impossible now that Ronan's face had betrayed his true feelings. Was this an answer to her prayers?

THIS WOULD BE A SURPRISE ATTACK. Ari Thorvaldsson cast a lingering glance at his family's chain-mail shirt, which he would leave behind to enable more stealth. His closest friend, Sigfrid, gave him a meaningful stare with his one functioning eye.

"What was the real purpose of this voyage, Ari?"

What sort of question was that? The entire crew understood his motivation to avenge his brother's blood, spilled in this deceptively green place—Ireland, some called it. The clan responsible for Egil's death must feel the wrath of the Northmen, as had so many others on this fair isle.

Feeling weighted by the heavy, humid air, Ari chose his weapon carefully and did not answer. He was most comfortable with his sword, its name carved in the blade: *Peacebreaker*. Surely it was an apt name, since peace had been stolen from him with Egil's untimely death. His brother had only been sixteen when he fell in a raid on this very castle.

Sigfrid pressed him again. "Are you certain you want to attack?"

A sudden twinge of doubt reared its head. He had only been ten himself when his brother was slain. His father forced him to stay with his mother on the longship, waiting for the outcome of the struggle. Although he could barely remember the castle his family had raided, he could still close his eyes and smell the pungent blood that had spread across Egil's chest that day.

His eyes fixed on the odd mountain backing this castle, its point similar to the beak of one of Odin's ravens. Strange that he could not recall it from his youth.

Sigfrid had not been with his family during that raid, so he could not confirm Ari's memory. But he had followed the course his father had mentioned, and the lines of the castle looked so familiar. This was the one.

Blond strands of hair escaped their leather binding as Ari nodded forcefully. "Of course we must attack. We did not sail here to trade or explore. We came for vengeance."

Sigfrid nodded. "Then take care as you scout for us."

Thunder boomed, and he sheathed Peacebreaker, taking his shorter knife in hand. This sharp angled *seax* would serve him well in close quarters. He hoped to gain access to the castle grounds before anyone could send up an alarm.

The men had set up camp last night and would soon lose the benefit of surprise. Ari knew they were still exhausted from the long voyage to this Irish inlet. He had to move now that twilight was falling.

He gave a nod to his men. No words were necessary. If they heard his battle cry, no force on earth could stop them, no matter how exhausted they were. Like a wave of heat and hatred, Vikings would sweep the offensive castle clean.

THE RAIN MOVED in heavy sheets, forming deep puddles and loosening Ari's footing. Creeping cautiously among the wet tangle of berry vines inside the walled garden, he hoped the tightly stitched seams of his leather boots would keep his feet dry. There was nothing he hated more than cold, soaked feet. At home, when he checked traps in the deep snows, there had been several times he'd feared frostbite would take his toes.

He glanced back at the circuitous route he'd taken to creep up to the rear of the castle. Clambering the stone wall hadn't been easy in the near dark, but it was surprisingly low. Perhaps the Irish were prepared for shorter invaders, or perhaps they anticipated attacks only on the castle gate in the front. He had spied but a single guard stationed there.

It was possible that he had timed his attack well, when the castle wasn't fully manned. And the crashing storm had provided effortless concealment. It was a sign: the gods smiled upon this raid.

He clenched his jaw. Who was he fooling? The gods hadn't protected his brother. They hadn't given him any happiness in the years he had tried to please his father, stepping into the position of heir. They had never even brought him a woman interesting enough to marry.

He fingered the ancient bronze bottle he kept belted inside his tunic. It was unwieldy, but it was his heritage, and he didn't want to die without it. It was a trophy from his ancestor, who had bravely sailed west, to this very country, and plundered the holy men who lived here. This bottle and its story had passed to each Thorvaldsson heir. Ari stomached the thought that Egil should have inherited it and pushed on.

Candlelight flickered in the window then disappeared. This was his chance. He gripped his seax, ready to slash at anyone inside. *For Egil,* he told himself. For Egil he would bring this castle to its knees.

CHAPTER 2

Spinning her mother's amber ring on her finger, Britta closed her eyes, picturing Ronan's intense gaze and how his sleek dark hair matched his neatly trimmed beard. Why had she never thought of him as a suitor? He was surely handsome, turning women's heads wherever he went.

Maybe it was because he talked to her as a friend—almost as one of the men. When he spoke with her father about taking animals to trade or building onto the castle, he had a way of pulling her into the conversation. Ronan took her opinions seriously; she was sure of that.

Florie rapped and opened the door, once again interrupting her musings. She stood just inside the room, awkwardly shifting on her feet. "Apologies if the oatcakes did not please."

Britta walked to her side, pulling her into a hug. She could never be angry with such a loyal friend.

"The oatcakes were tasty. Perhaps I used too much butter. My stomach has settled considerably."

Florie brightened.

Britta continued. "I wondered—has Ronan ever spoken to you about me?"

The nursemaid's freckled cheeks flooded with sudden color. "Well, now. I am not certain what you mean."

She was blunt. "Does he care for me, as more than just a friend?"

Florie hedged. "To be sure, he's never said a peep to me along those lines." She shot her a shrewd look. "But I've noticed he lets you win at the table games, which is contrary to his competitive nature. He also dashes outside the moment you announce you're taking a walk. And you remember the spring festival? There were so many eligible clansmen there, practically swarmin' around you. Ronan stayed right by your side, do you recall?"

She did. She had thought nothing of it at the time, because Ronan knew she was uncomfortable in large crowds and she'd assumed he was trying to set her at ease. Yet the way Florie described it, he had been protecting her from the advances of other men.

Abruptly, Florie moved toward the clattering shutters, giving a futile tug at the iron bar, which was already secure. "Listen to that driving rain! I'd better feed the guards now. They'll be soaked to the bone." She hurried from the room.

Florie's observations and her nervous behavior confirmed Britta's suspicions. Ronan did care for her. And what was wrong with that? He could read Latin. He loved God, as she did. He was well regarded by her father. Indeed, life with Ronan would be comfortable. But was it a comfortable life that God had called her to?

STOOPING, Ari silently rushed the side entry door. The dimming light of an oil lamp on the scullery wall indicated that someone had been here recently. He crept forward, thankful he hadn't worn the clinking chain mail.

A sense of echoing spaciousness met him as he passed through the next door. Embers died in a square hearth by the wall, casting long shadows. This must be the great hall. But where were the residents?

He sensed a movement to his right, but before he could turn to see if someone was there, a dull thud slammed into his stomach. A muffled cry jolted from his lips. Furious, Ari stabbed into the dark, in the direction of the attacker. Another blow fell, this time crushing his foot. Even as he tried to plunge farther, hot pain stabbed at his toes, driving him to the stone floor.

Not far away, a woman gave a horrified shout, filling the vaulted space. Ari tried to drag himself back to the doorway, but his long, large limbs would not respond. It was as if his crushed foot pinned his entire body to the ground.

Candles and lights surged toward him. He could make out the sturdy form of the woman who had screamed. She babbled in her native tongue, waving her hands like birds' wings. Three men drew closer, their lights forming a circle around him. A dark-haired man stooped to retrieve an object from the floor. Ari felt sick when he recognized the bronze spikes attached to a thick stick. He had been attacked with a mace. It was a wonder he had survived.

The man seemed to reprimand the older woman, who continued gesturing to the mace. She must have been the one who had flailed it at Ari, with all the ineptitude of a child wielding his first wooden sword. The bronze head of the mace was too heavy for her to handle, and she must have dropped it right on his foot. He realized the family bottle, tucked in his tunic, had deflected her first ill-placed blow to his chest. Otherwise his insides would have been mangled.

The dark-haired man was in charge, and he seemed to be pondering how to dispose of Ari in the most efficient manner. But the man's attentions were diverted when a single flickering candle moved down the stairs.

The golden light barely outlined a distinctly female form. As the woman approached, Ari sensed the power shifting from the dark-haired man to her. The circle of onlookers opened and she stepped forward, her black eyebrows raised in concern.

Slowly, she knelt by his side. Her feet crushed the lavender and rosemary strewn on the floor, releasing their scent afresh. The dark-haired man took her by the elbow and pulled her back to a standing position.

The older woman launched into her narrative again, only this time, she spoke slowly enough that Ari understood some of the words. His father owned Irish slaves, and he had listened closely and learned their language so he could converse with them. The woman seemed to be repeating the words *Northman* and *giant*. He grinned.

At this, the young woman with the tumbling black hair leaned in, holding the candle over Ari's chest. A hot drop of wax spattered onto his tunic, but he did not flinch, even as it burned his stomach.

The dark-haired man noted Ari's reaction, his face hardening.

As pain seared through his foot again, Ari curled up tighter, trying to relieve the pressure. He inwardly cursed himself for being reduced to such a position. Why didn't the man just run him through with his sword? Perhaps these Irish were torturers.

When he opened his eyes, a milk-white face hovered close. Fjord-blue eyes met his.

She spoke only one word, but it was a word he knew.

Healing.

BRITTA COULD NOT TEAR her eyes from the Northman. Even curled into a ball, it took all three guards and Ronan to move him to a pallet in her father's chamber upstairs. She had never seen a man so tall and large, saving perhaps Crim, son of the swineherd. And Crim was as filthy as his swine most of the time.

It was puzzling: She had been told that the Vikings were dirty, crawling with bugs and reeking like the corpses of their victims. This man's clothing was not unkempt, and his skin and hair were not foul. Only the faint scent of smoke clung to him.

The hulking blond man had remained mostly quiet until one of the guard's hands accidentally slipped from his shin to his bloody foot. He unleashed a roar that nearly made the guards drop him, and she could not restrain her gasp.

Ronan's eyes were steely as he deposited the Viking, none too gently, on the pallet. He had not approved of her suggestion to rehabilitate the man before her father returned to execute judgment. She had to admit, Ronan's idea of a swift death might be the better plan. The Viking's eyes flashed with unconcealed hatred, and she knew he brought an unprecedented threat to their peaceful inlet.

Yet when his pale, blue-silver eyes paused on hers, his candid gaze spoke louder than words. He longed for certainty, as she did. Perhaps even some kind of redemption. This man had a soul, no matter how brutal his culture was.

Thankfully, Florie knew much about healing, not only because she had nursed many injured clansmen over the years, but because her own husband was an invalid. She would do as Britta asked, despite her fear of the Viking.

Britta grimaced, imagining Florie swinging Ronan's mace blindly in the dark. How had she managed to maim the intruder enough to halt his attack? God must have guided her hands.

The guards nodded at Britta as they took their leave. Ronan walked toward her, placing a light hand on her shoulder and fixing his eyes on hers. She couldn't be sure if they blazed with desire or fierce protectiveness.

"You're certain you want to keep him alive? He seems a beast."

"Yes. Father will want to know if there are more Vikings coming to our shores. Perhaps we can find a way to communicate with him."

After considering, Ronan finally gave a half nod, as if this were a sound reason. "A guard will stand at his door for the duration of his stay."

She knew this would leave them short a guard at the castle gate. She summoned false courage. "I have my own knife, and so does Florie. We will require no extra protection."

Ronan laughed softly. "After seeing how Florie handled my mace, I shudder to think what she would do with a knife. Clancy will be posted outside his door."

The Viking groaned, his body curled toward the wall. Florie would soon arrive with the herbs and cloths to wrap his foot. Perhaps they could offer him warm broth, if he understood they meant well.

But if he did not understand… Britta shivered.

CHAPTER 3

It was only a matter of time before his men would come looking. Ari could not decide which would be better: if his crew stormed the castle or if Sigfrid came alone. If they attacked the castle, his mission would be fulfilled because these murdering Irishmen would be dead.

But his thoughts lurched unwillingly to the beautiful goddess who had devoted herself to his care. The raven-haired, plush-lipped maiden had not ceased trying to coax words from him. Did she suspect how well he understood her language? He had determined to feign ignorance, to be the heathen wild man they seemed to think him. He would not become attached in any way to the family who killed Egil.

Yet the young woman—*Britta* is what they called her—would sit and read aloud to him after the nursemaid changed the herbal wraps on his foot. He supposed she was trying to distract him from his continued pain.

Three days had passed, and his swollen foot had shifted from a deep red to shades of purple and green. The barbed spikes of the mace had left open wounds, but they had begun to heal. The deeper throbbing was what tested his fortitude. But the tea the nursemaid brought regularly—it tasted of willow bark—seemed to ease the pressure.

Ari finally determined that the book Britta read from was her holy book. She treated the thick leather binding, with its numerous vellum pages, with utmost care. He had heard there was a holy book like this not far from his home in Norway, displayed in a newly built Christian church. He had not seen it, because his family would not approve if he went there. They spat upon the ways of Jesus Christ, determined to cling to Odin, Thor, Freyja, and so many others.

Even as Britta devoted hours to his care, the dark-haired man—he seemed to be called *Ronan*—spent most of his time pinning him with blazing looks. There was no doubt the Irishman wanted him dead. Ari closely watched Ronan's movements and moods. Perhaps he was the one who had killed his brother. Ari could probably overpower him, once he was able to walk.

Today, Ronan swept into the room, shooing the guard from the door and leaning over Britta as she read. He spoke so rapidly to her, Ari could only decipher one word: *Viking*. The book she cradled dropped to her lap. She looked at Ari, then back at Ronan.

What had the heartless troll told her?

RONAN'S WORDS TUMBLED OUT, unharnessed and unsoftened. "A Viking horde camps by the mouth of our inlet. I have watched them as they sit about, sharpening horrible axes and knives...gleaming swords like the one this fellow had. They are heavily armed, and with so many, they could take this castle in just a few moments. We must either send this man back, kill him, or send an emissary of goodwill."

The Bible dropped into her lap with a thud, but Britta barely felt it. So many Vikings already encamped. Ronan had been wrong to trust her judgment. She had failed her O'Shea name. And what now? Would her father even be able to return home with those savages encamped so close by?

Yet a glance at the Viking told her he was not as savage as Ronan would have her believe. The man had taken food gratefully from her hand and had allowed Florie to place cool cloths and herbs on his wounds. He had watched as she turned pages, slowly sounding out Latin words as she pointed to the symbols.

But she could understand Ronan's nervousness, given that the Viking watched his every move like a lion waiting to pounce. His hatred was not veiled as it burned in those sea-colored eyes. Britta suspected that like Ronan, the Viking was a fearsome warrior, and both men sensed a worthy opponent.

Ronan caught the Viking looking at her. "I can make it easy for him," he whispered. "A knife to his throat as he sleeps and he would not feel pain."

She drew back. As a warrior, Ronan was surely capable of such violence, but he must see it was morally wrong to kill an unarmed man.

She controlled her voice, lowering it for emphasis. "You have given me three choices—to send him back, to kill him, or to send an emissary. His foot is still weak, and it needs more care than they will be able to provide in a makeshift camp, so he cannot return to them yet. As far as killing him, you know I cannot condone the murder of an injured man who cannot defend himself. So I will choose the last option—sending an emissary to the Vikings." She paused, forcing herself to say the next words. "And I will be that emissary."

ARI WATCHED as Ronan's words grew heated. Although he gestured wildly in the air, it was clear he would not lay a hand on Britta. The two seemed to reach a tentative agreement, and the powerful man strode out the door.

She resumed her position, sitting back in the gold-studded chair by his pallet and picking up her holy book. She chose a page and began to read, but he interrupted her, croaking out a word for the first time in days.

"Ari." He pointed to his chest and repeated it, louder. "Ari."

She hesitated, her huge blue eyes searching his.

He nodded and said it again, motioning to himself. "Ari."

She leaned forward—if Ronan were here, Ari knew he would reprove her for a lack of caution, and Ari wouldn't blame him. She was altogether too trusting.

"Britta," she said, resting a pale hand on her embroidered ivory dress.

He repeated the word, enjoying the way it sounded with his heavy accent. "Bree-ta."

Her gaze returned to her book, and she seemed lost in her own thoughts. Finally, she pointed to a word next to a hand-drawn picture of a room filled with golden goblets and their holy cross symbol. "Mon-a-ster-i-um," she said, drawing out each sound.

It was a long word, but perhaps he needed to show her he was grateful for her daily teaching, even though the word she spoke was a reminder of the divide between her people and his. His ancestors had attacked such monasteries to gain the wealth needed to secure their power. Even now, his bronze heirloom bottle was hidden on the floor beneath his pallet, one side of it bearing a slight indentation from the misplaced blow of the mace. He would not leave this place without it.

With effort, his rough voice sounded out, "Mun-e-sterrr-i-um."

The smile that spread over Britta's face replaced all the

anxiety that had clouded it when she exchanged words with Ronan. Ari wished he could think of other ways to make her smile.

LEAVING Ari in Florie's capable, but still somewhat-resistant hands, Britta hurried to her room to change out of her ivory dress. She wanted to wear something that would indicate her position as princess.

Although her father's kingdom was small, it was well respected. It was quite an arduous journey over the hills for Father to discuss matters with the high king, and he only went twice a year. She hated that this was one of those times. She never knew how long such travels might take—once, he had stayed for a full month.

She hoped her actions would please her father, but deep inside, she was fairly certain that he would have agreed with Ronan and disposed of the Viking invader, instead of allowing the injured man to rest on a pallet in his room.

Shaking such doubts from her mind, she donned a tea-colored silk dress with pink roses scattered over the skirt. She placed a narrow, braided, golden crown on her head.

For good measure, she pulled up her skirts and strapped a belt around her waist. Attached to the belt was a long sheath she tied in place on her thigh. From a drawer next to her bed, she retrieved her antler-handled dagger and carefully slid it into the sheath. She hoped the Vikings would not attack her when they realized she carried no sword, but if she were captured, at least she would have a secret weapon.

Yet her best weapon was Ronan, who had refused to let her approach the encampment alone. It was a foolish thing for him to come along, because if they were both killed, the castle would fall. True, he would place one of the guards in charge, but no guard was as vigilant and deadly as Ronan.

As she descended the stairs, she watched to make sure the chunky dagger handle did not protrude beneath her skirts. Realization struck her—how would she communicate with the heathen warriors? Hand gestures could prove deadly if they were misunderstood.

Perhaps Ari could teach her what to say, something that would make her peaceful intent clear.

She turned, hoping she could trust the Northman to share a word that would protect the castle, instead of one that called for an attack.

CHAPTER 4

Florie met her in the stairwell, her pink face anxious. "M'lady, I was just coming to fetch you. He's gaining strength in his foot, 'tis certain. He's trying to hide it from us."

Britta could not be distracted. Even now, Ronan was probably putting on his mail shirt and gathering his weapons. She patted Florie's hand. "We will watch him closely. For now, he will go nowhere—our guard Clancy stands just outside the door, and he is wider than the Viking. Do not fret."

Florie tucked stray wisps of hair beneath her kerchief and straightened her apron. "As you say, m'lady. I've dressed his foot, so I'll be going down to prepare our meal." She paused, her gaze trailing from Britta's crown to her nicer clothing. "Have you dressed early for the evening meal?"

"Ronan and I will be traveling today." Britta did not elaborate. Much as she longed to tell her nursemaid about her dangerous mission so she could savor some motherly sympathy, she would not allow herself to do it. Florie had already risked her own life, attacking the invader in the dark with a mace.

What would she do if she realized the princess herself planned to stride into a Viking war camp? Britta could just envision Florie, her stout form clad in a man's mail shirt, spear in hand, accompanying her charge. She hid a smile. No, her loyal Florie must not know her plan.

As she entered the room, Ari turned his gaze from the window to her. His curious yet appreciative glance swept over her royal clothing and crown. Knowing she had no time to waste, she rifled through her stack of books on the floor, searching for one she had read many times.

When she found the volume she wanted, she searched out a particular picture in it then held it up for Ari to see. His cool eyes moved across the colorful page. It portrayed two armies facing off, but their weapons were no longer drawn. Two men met in the middle, helmets in hand. One carried a stick with a white cloth tied to it. They were obviously seeking a truce.

She pointed to the page where the two men stood. "Peace," she said, hoping he understood.

He gave her a blank stare. Did the Vikings have no concept of peace? It would certainly fit with the stories she'd been told as a child. The Northmen were villains who slipped onto Irish shores in dragon-head ships, killing to take what they wanted, stealing natives to make them slaves. There was nothing fair about the Viking attacks, no chance to be armed against a force that was nearly invisible until the last minute.

But she *must* have something to say to the Viking men in the camp. True, she could bring along one of Ari's things, like his sword, or the bottle he'd tried to hide under his pallet, but then the Vikings might assume he had already died at their hand. If so, surely their wrath would be swift.

With renewed fervor, she tapped at the men in the picture. Then she placed the book on her lap and rammed her fists together to indicate fighting. Finally, she abruptly pulled her hands apart, holding them upright to show that the warring sides were at peace.

"Peace," she repeated, praying for a word, just one word, that could save her family home.

Recognition sparked in Ari's face, and his lips slid into a half smile. He spoke carefully: "Greethe."

She repeated the word several times. When Ari nodded in approval, she placed her book on the floor then stood and hurried from the room.

AS THE DOOR slammed behind Britta, Ari flexed his foot, pondering. She had been carefully dressed as royalty, and she had asked him how to say *grið*, the Norse word for peace. Although his thoughts were sluggish from something in the tea, he sat bolt upright as he began to understand.

She was going to see his men. She was going to ask for peace. That was the only explanation for her behavior.

How would Sigfrid react to Britta's approach? Thankfully, Ari's second-in-command never acted rashly, but when he determined someone was a threat, he would not hesitate to crush them.

Ari could not let his crew fall upon the helpless, trusting woman who had kept watch over him for days. He felt beneath his pallet, hoping they had not taken the knife he had hidden there, but it was gone. His eyes widened as he realized his heirloom bottle was also missing. The tea must have made him sleep through their pilfering. But why would they take something of no value to them?

He allowed his fear for Britta to flow through him. It washed away thoughts of the bottle and subdued the throbbing, heavy pain in his foot. Determined, he pulled his leg to the side of the pallet, allowing his foot to touch the floor for the first time since his injury. Although he could hardly bend his ankle, he tried to rotate his stiff foot before grabbing the back of the chair and pulling himself to a standing position.

The foot gave way, and he let out a light groan, which he quickly stifled. If he had to crawl to Britta's side, he would. Sigfrid would see him and stay his attack plans until he gave the word.

Someone shifted outside the door. Doubtless, they had left a guard behind. Where was his sword? Glancing around, he realized that not only had they taken his weapons, they had also taken his boots.

The still-swollen foot needed support. Unwilling to bend to the level of the low pallet, he struggled to take his tunic off then ripped into the bottom of the linen with his teeth. He managed to tear off a strip of cloth and wrap it around his foot. Each move was agonizing, but he could not give up. Wrestling his way back into his tunic, he scowled at the sight of his half-exposed stomach. It still bore a deep bruise from the impact of the mace on the bottle. Sigfrid would fear the worst had happened to him. But there was no time to search for another tunic.

His only advantage over the guard was the ability to surprise. He haltingly shuffled to the door, senses alert. The man outside sniffled then sneezed. Ari could only hope he was weakened with an illness.

An image of Britta, her pale cheeks flushing as she met his eyes, sprang to mind. If his men killed her, he would never forgive himself.

Gathering his strength, he pulled up the latch on the heavy wooden door, thankful it locked from inside. In one fluid move, he yanked the door back, thrusting his body forward to assault the unwitting guard.

Too late he realized that there were only two long steps between the landing and the first steep stair. When he collided with the large Irish guard's frame, he knocked them both into the darkened stone stairwell. Their bodies plummeted onto the jutting steps, tumbling over one another.

Fresh pain gave him a light head, and when they reached the bottom step, Ari's world went black.

CHAPTER 5

When Britta met Ronan in the great hall, she was not surprised to see that he was wearing his long mail shirt. His sword was sheathed, and he carried his mace over one shoulder. Trying to look at him as the Vikings would, she imagined he would seem like a regular demon, with his blazing eyes and red wool clothing.

She rested her hand on her friend's arm. "We must first pray."

Ronan nodded, taking the lead. "May the shield of God protect us from these pagans. May the angels of God give us protection. And may Christ be over all. Amen."

She felt safer walking toward the unknown with this God-fearing demon Irishman at her side. Their steps echoed as they entered the stone courtyard outside the entryway. The morning was brisk, and the cold air made her wish she had donned her woolen cape. But she wanted to appear unarmed to the Northmen.

Ronan led the way through the plush green grass, around the small streams she knew so well. She tried to forget her mission, noting how the clouds cast shadows and patterns on their hills.

But after they climbed the final rise, she gasped. The field that edged the rocky gray coastline was dotted with drab-colored tents—at least twenty of them.

Farther off, where the grass gave way to the shoreline, they had dug a semicircular earthen rampart, blocking their long, dragon-prowed ships from easy attack. At least ten fully armed men guarded the dirt blockade.

As they drew closer, smells of cooking fish assailed them. The Northmen themselves struck her as incredibly hairy, with beards and fur vests and long, wild hair. Each one seemed to have several weapons on his belt.

These were barbarians indeed, handily shaping the land to their own purposes and sleeping outside in the elements. They were rough and rugged as the stags on Crow Mountain.

Ronan grasped her arm. "You do not have to be the one, Britta."

She shook her head. "Indeed I do. You cannot enter their camp alone. They will see you as a threat because you *are* a threat. You cannot hide the passion shining in your eyes—you would like to see them all dead."

He looked to the camp and nodded. "You are correct. But you must admit it is wise to be distrustful of these heathen. You have read the stories, Britta, and you have heard our monks' fearful prayer: 'From the fury of the Northmen, deliver us, O Lord.' These Northmen have ravaged our shores for so many years, I am certain they intend to plunder our castle." He paused, his russet eyes searching hers. "Your blond invalid is no innocent. He came to vanquish us—make no mistake. I see the passion in *his* eyes."

Britta could not deny it was true. Occasionally when he wasn't watching her, she noticed how a strange sadness would darken Ari's countenance. It was as if he were pining for someone. Was it a woman from his homeland? Perhaps a wife?

She shook off her doubts, pointing to a leather-clad, grizzle-bearded man who had silently moved toward them. When they glanced his way, he leaned on a tall spear, affecting carelessness. "It is too late to argue over this. They have already seen us."

With feigned boldness, she strode toward the man, holding her crowned head high. She could feel Ronan's solid bulk moving directly behind her.

About three feet from the scar-faced warrior, she stopped short and gathered herself to her full height, which apparently didn't amount to much. The Northmen towered over her as they began to form a semicircle around their leader. Their hands hung by their sides, but they had easy access to the sharpened swords and axes on their belts.

She closed her eyes, asking God to help her. Then she focused on the leader's one clear eye, since the other was merely a sightless, tight-lidded slit. "Greethe," she said slowly.

The man's lips twitched, and his gaze sharpened. She repeated the word.

Ever watchful, Ronan stood in silence slightly to her left. If any Northman moved her way, she would need to drop so Ronan's mace could hit him square in the head. He would follow that strike with a sword thrust to the gut.

The Northman scratched at his rough beard. "Greethe?" he asked.

She nodded. Hoping it was not a mistake, she slowly withdrew Ari's bronze bottle from a silken pouch she had tied to her belt. Taking a step closer to the obviously unwashed man, she held the bottle out to him, cupped in her palms. "Greethe."

The man snatched the bottle from her before Ronan could step between them. He spat out a string of clipped words to his men.

She caught one of the words and repeated it. "Ari." She put on a cheerful smile, trying to indicate that the Viking was healthy and alive. But how could she show them he lay abed, without leading them to believe he had died?

A stick lying in the dirt caught her eye, and she saw her opportunity. She slowly bent to pick it up. Silence fell upon the skittish Northmen. Ronan glided a step forward so he was at her side.

She took the stick and carved into the damp soil. It was slow going, but she was finally able to depict a rectangular castle with a jutting mountain behind it. Then she drew the sea and cliffs on the other side and scratches to indicate the camp. Finally, she drew a deliberate, deep line between the castle and the campsite. Her voice was firm and steady as she said, "Greethe." She tapped her crown to bring attention to her authority.

For a long moment, the bearded man did not respond. He gripped the bronze bottle tightly as he examined her dirt drawing. When he looked up, she slowed her erratic breathing so she could meet his gaze. Instead, the man fixed his eye on Ronan. Some wordless understanding passed between the men, and Ronan did not react when the Northman extended the bottle toward her.

"Ari," he said, his voice charged with concern.

She nodded, wrapping the cold bottle in her hands. Comfort flooded her. God had spared her life, and she would be able to return the vessel to its rightful owner. She let her voice soften as she said, "Ari. Greethe."

Ronan's hand squeezed her shoulder as he brusquely steered her away from the circle of Vikings. A truce had obviously been reached. The Northmen would not attack while Ari was within the castle walls.

But from the wild look in the Viking warriors' eyes, Britta knew the truce would end the moment Ari rejoined his crew.

She must find a way to delay him until her father returned home with his soldiers.

CHAPTER 6

Shifting on the rough board he rested on, Ari tried to recall what had happened after he attacked his guard.

Memories flitted around like swirling seabirds. He caught snatches of images: the Irish guard nursing a bloody lip, the sheath of the man's sword banging into his leg, and the pain that finally tore into his foot like a wild berserker charging his enemy. When the heavy guard's full weight had landed on Ari's wounded foot, the agony had knocked him senseless.

He could slightly remember two men moving him to a side room on the ground floor. They had placed him, none too carefully, onto a low board resting on two wooden blocks. A rough wool blanket was tossed over him, and they left, locking the door behind them.

Now it was night, given the darkness and the dim moonlight trickling through the high window. As he cautiously bent to touch his twisted foot, a metallic sound captured his attention. Someone was fumbling at the latch. He lowered back to the board, pretending to be asleep as he watched through narrowed eyes. A dark figure noiselessly stepped into the room, hastening to his bedside. The person leaned in close, as if listening for movement.

It was impossible to discern if the shape was male or female. But if it were Britta or Florie, wouldn't she speak up? The stillness grew heavy and ominous. He tried to slow his breathing, but his heart thudded like a bucking stallion. He could feel the intruder's breath on his face.

He could bear it no longer. He shoved his hand out and wrapped it around the person's throat—a thick throat, surely a man's—when the sharp tang of a knife blade pinched the skin on his own neck.

He tightened his grip. "No knife," he said, using Irish words.

Pressure from the knife lessened; then as he squeezed harder, the weapon dropped onto the blanket. Immediately, he shoved himself upward, slamming his forehead into the intruder's jaw and knocking the man backward.

As the man groaned, Ari flung himself from the bed, directly onto the prone form. He pinned him to the ground.

"Halt." The man's rough command was easily recognized—it was Ronan. The Irishman had tried to kill him.

Lantern light shone into the room and Britta appeared in the doorway, unable to see them. She stood there, her white gown peeping from beneath a long, embroidered wrap.

Casting her light about until it fell upon the men, her voice rose in concern. "Ari! Ronan? What has happened? I heard noises. Did someone enter the castle?"

Ari rolled off the Irishman, glaring at the man as he grabbed the knife. He pointed the knife tip at Ronan. "This man tried to slay me."

"No." Her eyes flashed and color flushed her cheeks as she turned to Ronan. "Surely you did not?"

Ronan grunted. "Your father would have wanted it—in fact, I am sure he would have commanded this Viking's death the moment he stole into our castle. He has brought nothing but trouble to us. You have examined our valiant guard Clancy's arm after his tumble down the stairs, and you know his fracture will take many days to heal. We are left with only two guards and myself to defend these walls, should the Northmen invade. We will fall, Princess."

Unwilling to believe Ari had deliberately injured the guard, Britta boldly extended her open hand for Ronan's knife. Ari glanced at Ronan, then at her. Acknowledging her authority with a slight drop of his chin, he carefully placed the weapon in her hand.

She helped Ronan to his feet and handed him his knife. "Leave us for a moment. You can see he means me no harm."

Ronan's dark glare fell on Ari as he rubbed his reddened neck. "It is not wise. I cannot leave you alone with this unpredictable rogue."

"It is an order. I have the final say in my father's absence." Her feet were planted and determination charged her words.

Ronan strode to the door. His voice was thick with emotion. "I will stand outside, but the door will stay cracked. If you so much as breathe my name, he is a dead man. Be cautious, Britta."

Ari sensed the tenderness Ronan used when he spoke her name. The man cared for her—perhaps even loved her.

As the door began to close, Britta moved to Ari's side. It was not hard to imagine how the Irishman had fallen for her. Her touch was soft, yet firm, as she cupped his elbow and helped him to his feet. As he stretched to his full height, he realized that although she had such an imposing presence, she was far shorter than he. Despite her curves, she was compact. In fact, he could pick her up with one hand and throw her over his shoulder...

Where were these thoughts coming from? He was thinking like a lovestruck fool, like a man starved for affection.

Maybe he was.

As he looked down into her earnest blue eyes, he fought his base urge to lower his chin and cover her full, half-parted lips with his own.

She seemed to sense his intent, but instead of drawing back, she stood still, as if transfixed. He restrained himself and waited for her to speak.

She cleared her throat and spoke slowly. "I saw your men today." She withdrew his bottle from under her wrap and handed it to him. "I also wanted to return this to you."

He fingered its familiar bronze shape, always cool to the touch. It felt a bit gritty with patina and could use a good polish. He looked at the daring princess, acknowledging what she had said.

"My men?"

She nodded, covering one eye with her hand. "Your one-eyed man agreed on a truce, at least for now."

"Sigfrid," he said, incredulous. He had unwittingly thrown himself down a flight of stairs to protect Britta from approaching this very warrior. Yet without his aid, she had secured a truce with the battle-hardened man.

She looked shyly at the floor.

Who was this woman who carried such magical charm?

BRITTA BRACED HER FEET, trying to restrain herself from taking a step toward the tall Viking.

It was as if her senses were only attuned to his presence. No other smell mattered, save his leathery scent. No other sight mattered, save her upward view of his neat blond beard and ocean-colored eyes. No other sound mattered, save the husky tones of his words.

Standing so close, her senses conspired against her, pulling her toward him like invisible cords. She had read love poems in her books, but nothing had prepared her for the sheer physical force the emotion carried.

Even so, her head told her that love was more than an emotion. It was a commitment, such as Florie had with her husband, James, who had been sick in bed with the coughing, consumptive disease for almost two years now. He was useless at maintaining their small stone house, and they had to hire a boy to keep up with farm chores.

As Ari began to lower himself onto the board bed, she extended a hand to help. Her guards had given her little say in their decision to move Ari into this room. Once they saw Clancy's broken arm, they determined the volatile pagan could not remain in the king's chamber. Besides, he had already rolled downstairs, which made it easier for them.

As he settled back, she voiced the question weighing on her. "Why did you try to escape? Did we not treat you kindly?"

Ari's forehead wrinkled. "Yes, kindness. It was not escape—I went to aid you. With my men."

Britta caught her breath. He'd intended to accompany her, even though it was a fool's errand—he couldn't have walked all the way to the Viking camp.

"You worried about my safety?"

In answer, Ari took her hand in his own. Unable to look away, she stared at his strong arm, covered in blond hairs and a sinuous dragon tattoo. She allowed herself to savor the feel of his large, rough palm, gripping her own small hand.

"Yes." His eyes searched hers.

Unable to speak, she startled at the sound of shuffling shoes and deep voices in the great hall. Ari quickly released her hand. She stole to the door, peering out the crack.

Men moved around the great hall. Sensing Ronan's presence outside the doorway, she boldly edged forward, watching torchlight illuminate their features. Catching sight of a familiar face, she gave a short cry and pushed forward into the hall.

"Father!"

CHAPTER 7

Britta threw herself into her father's outstretched arms. She clung to him, even though the small metal links of his chain mail shirt pressed into her exposed neckline. She pulled back to get a good look at him. His hair, streaked with white and gray, was trimmed and thick. He had not lost weight on his journey. His gray eyes twinkled. Things must have gone well with the high king—but hopefully not so well he had betrothed her to one of the princes.

"I see you have missed me, Daughter?"

She hugged him again, unwilling to be separated from him yet. "Indeed. The castle was empty without you."

Behind her, she heard Ronan slide the bolt across Ari's wide-planked door before stepping from the shadows. A heavy weight seemed to drop into her stomach as she waited for him to mention their Viking prisoner.

"Welcome, m'lord. Indeed, we are glad to see your safe return. I understand it is deep into the night, but we must discuss several things."

Father's face grew serious. "Of course." He motioned to his

weary men. "Disperse to your own homes tonight. Tomorrow evening we will gather here for a feast."

Britta followed her father and Ronan upstairs, relieved she would have the chance to explain her actions to Father. But outside Father's chamber door, Ronan shooed her away.

Anger sparked through her, and she felt her eyes widen. "I am not some servant you can whisk away, Ronan. I am the king's daughter."

Father turned and gave her a thoughtful look. "Indeed you are. But whatever Ronan has to say, I am certain it is as one warrior to another. You can speak with me in the morning, but now you must get your rest."

Much as she longed to dig in her heels and explain what had occurred in his absence, Britta had learned long ago not to cross her father when he took that tone. He would not listen to a word she said and, in fact, would be more likely to go against her wishes.

Plodding into her room, she draped her midnight-blue embroidered wrap over a chair and tumbled into her bed. Pulling the heavy bed curtains shut, she yanked the blankets up around her. She wished her fire had not burned down to coals. Sometimes the wind seemed to prod through every chink in the castle walls, pushing the chill right into her bones.

Despite her exhaustion from her meeting with the Vikings, sleep would not claim her. After trying unsuccessfully to get comfortable, Britta finally drew the curtains, lit her candle, and picked up a book near her bed.

As she read the tale of a mythical hero who fought sea robbers, she found herself picturing Ari. She remembered the long, intimidating ships docked near the Viking camp. It was easy to imagine the tall Northman, his blond beard shining in the sunlight, sleeves pushed up to show his tattoo, as he sailed to conquer new lands.

But this was her land. And she did not want it conquered.

Despite her growing attraction to Ari, if she allowed herself to look at the situation dispassionately, she knew he had not changed his intentions since he stole into the great hall. Ronan knew this, too.

Would Ronan recommend execution to her father? And was there any reason for her to stand against it, since not only was her life at stake, but the lives of everyone in her father's kingdom?

❖

THE CASTLE FORCES HAD RETURNED; Ari was sure of it.

His foot was stiff from the cold, so he could not creep to the door to observe, but the clamor of deep voices told him all he needed to know.

Britta seemed oblivious to his true intentions. Hadn't he come to kill everyone, to bring revenge for his brother's untimely death? He could never forget the turbulent emotions of that battle-torn day in Ireland so many years ago. He could never wipe away his mother's lifelong loss and his father's deep grief over the death of his firstborn.

He had come to make things right, not to become entangled with an Irish princess he could not give his heart to. When he healed—if they allowed him to leave—he and his men could attack, and this loathsome castle would be destroyed. How many years had he longed to tear it apart, stone by stone? To torch its wooden support timbers and watch it burn?

His room had no fire, so his thin clothing was altogether inadequate. He drew his blanket tighter. The stiff board beneath him made it impossible to become comfortable, and he was sure that had been the guards' intent. Until now, they had been meticulous with his care. After his bungled attempt to protect the princess, which must have resulted in an injury to one of their men, they would be wary and give him no sympathy.

Except for Britta, who seemed tethered to him somehow. She was not put off by his size, his people, or his violence.

A new voice seemed to penetrate his heart—a truthful voice that seemed older than time itself. The voice said only one word, but he heard it very clearly: *hope*.

◆

FROM HER WINDOW SEAT, Britta watched the muted pinks and yellows of sunrise seeping across the deep blue inlet. Seeing God's hand as He painted the world made her feel refreshed and composed. Perhaps Father and Ronan had decided on a reasonable course of action for Ari.

But her tranquility was undone as Florie entered her room, her words tumbling out. "I've already laid the morning meal for your father and Ronan. They will have many actions to carry out before the feast. I thought to myself, p'raps you might want to catch them first."

Understanding what Florie had left unspoken—that judgment would fall on Ari today—Britta sprang into motion, throwing off her nightclothes and pulling a red brocade dress from her wardrobe. Red was not her favorite color, but she had no time to stop and think. She must catch Father before he spoke to Ari.

Florie aided her, tightening the laces in the back. "You haven't been eating enough, 'tis sure, m'lady. But we'll have fresh meat tonight and one of those apple pastries you love so much."

The last thing she cared about was food, but she turned, taking Florie's round face in her hands. She planted a kiss on each cheek. "Thank you for looking after me, Florie. I know you are stretched thin with your James abed."

Florie shook her head. "There's naught I can do for him that I haven't already done. Looking after you and your family gives me a purpose, and James wants me over here, not clucking over him like a mother hen."

Britta squeezed her nursemaid's hand, hoping to derive a last measure of strength before she approached her father downstairs. As she pulled on her slippers and walked out of the room, Florie called after her. "May God fill you with hope, m'lady."

Hope. An invisible comfort that seemed oceans away. The Viking tide that had washed onto their shore carried with it only one promise: dread. And her father wouldn't tolerate it.

◈

RONAN AND FATHER were so deep in conversation, they paid no heed to Britta as she descended into the great hall. Only when she sat next to her father and tapped his arm did he look at her.

"My dearest." He brushed her cheek with a kiss then took a small bite of his cabbage pie.

Ronan's gaze fell heavily upon her, full of conflicted emotions.

Her heart sank. She took up her spoon, absently tapping the shell of her soft-boiled egg.

Father spoke into the awkward silence. "Ronan has told me of the Vikings, and of this *Ari* who has enjoyed our hospitality although he arrived with evil intent. What have you to say to this, Daughter?"

Ronan spoke before she could reply. "I explained how we decided Ari was not a danger to us." His deep brown eyes held hers, imploring her to play along.

So Ronan had taken the blame for her own lapse in judgment. Probably for Clancy's resulting injury, as well. Her heart swelled with gratefulness.

She shared what Ari had told her. "Ari did not try to harm Clancy. He wanted to accompany me when I spoke to his men."

"To trap you, I shouldn't wonder," Father mused.

"No, he feared his man would try to harm me. I think he feels protective of me."

Her father shifted so he could look at her directly. "So he *says*, Britta. But a man will say anything to escape his prison, comfortable as it might be. No. I will speak to him myself and discern his motives."

She felt like spitting out the bite of chewy egg she had taken. Was Father right? Had Ari lied to her? He seemed so earnest, but she had only run across one liar in her life, and that was a mouthy chimney sweep her father had released from service before he had even finished his job.

After the men finished eating, she stood with them and filed into Ari's small room. If nothing else, she would be nearby when her father passed sentence on the Viking.

CHAPTER 8

Ari was thankful for the fresh clothing Florie had brought him, even though the green tunic was a bit small and stretched along his shoulders. After her early morning ministrations with warm cloths and fresh linen strips for his foot, he felt strong enough to risk standing on it again. Despite the bruising, he could tell it had healed somewhat.

When the door opened, he sank quickly to the board. He did not want to let anyone know the speed of his recovery.

An older man stepped into the room, his gray eyes solemn. He wore a rich purple velvet tunic embroidered with a family crest. A heavy gold cross pendant hung from his neck. This was their leader, Ari was certain.

Ronan stood alongside the powerful older man, and Britta hung back, her gaze flickering from Ari's foot to his face.

The man spoke. "I am King Kacey O'Shea, ruler of this land, and Britta's father. You have come to our shore with plans for an attack. How do you answer?"

Ari understood most of the man's thickly accented words, like *ruler*, *father*, and *attack*, but when he paused expectantly, Ari realized he had missed some question. He looked helplessly at Britta.

To the obvious discomfort of both men, she walked confidently to Ari's side. She leaned toward him and spoke slowly. "Why did you come to Ireland?"

A lie would be easy and might spare his life. But there was no honor in a liar.

"Avenge my brother's death...killed on a raid of your castle."

Britta's eyes clouded, but she nodded that she understood.

"Blood for blood," he added.

As she explained to the men, her hands fluttered nervously. Dark hair slipped around her cheeks, but it did not hide the tears glistening in her eyes. She, too, feared the decision of her father.

Perhaps this was his chance to escape. Could he overpower both the king and Ronan before bolting for the door? He hesitated. The older man looked perplexed. He spoke rapidly to Ronan, and both seemed to agree. He turned and spoke to his daughter, but this time Ari understood every word.

"Vikings have not come to our shores before. It was not this castle. He is mistaken."

◈

BRITTA KNEW Ari must have recognized the truth in her father's words, because he fell silent. When he finally spoke to her, the dangerous spark that had burned in his eyes was all but quenched.

"I feared this. The mountain...not the same as when I was young."

Her heart clenched. So Ari had been in Ireland alongside his brother when he was killed. She fought the urge to hug his shoulders, which were straining at the seams of his undersized tunic. Instead, she placed her hand briefly on his arm.

Immediately, Father shot her a sharp look. "Britta—"

He was interrupted by a guard's sudden appearance in the room. The breathless man's words were clipped.

"A rider came. King Tynan's lands have already fallen. The Normans have invaded."

❖

Normans! Britta had heard of these clever, greedy men. Skilled in both rhetoric and military tactics, they were practically unstoppable in their conquests. In fact, the Normans were descended from the Northmen but had married the French and changed loyalties. They served no one but themselves.

King Tynan's realm was to their east. It was impossible to believe that it had fallen, with the king's extensive forces. There would be no hope for her father's smaller kingdom. The Normans would rule over her family and reduce them to peasants. Soon all of Ciar's Kingdom would belong to the invaders.

Ari continued to sit in his own stunned silence while Ronan and Father spoke with the messenger. She could not bear to hear the fear in their voices. The feast tonight would not be a time of celebration, but of preparation for war.

Suddenly, Ari's determined, booming voice echoed from the stone walls in the small room.

"I must speak with my people."

Father stared at him, obviously shocked by the impertinence of his demand.

Ronan did not hold his tongue. "Pray tell us, why?"

Ari turned to Britta, his pensive eyes searching her face. But he returned his gaze to her father, palms outstretched as if beseeching him for mercy. He began to string more Irish words together than he ever had before, which made her wonder if he had understood more of their private conversations than she'd suspected.

"I have wronged you...acted dishonorably. I rallied my crew for revenge, then led them to the wrong castle. My hatred blinded me."

Britta glanced at the men. Ronan looked dubious, but Father seemed convinced by what Ari had said.

He continued. "I must ask you to let me return to my men and tell them of my foolish mistake."

"But you cannot walk!" Ronan spat out.

Before she knew what was happening, Ari rose to his feet beside her. His jaw was clenched in concentration, and when he swayed a little, she grabbed his forearm to support him. He took two steps toward the men, and Ronan's hand dropped to his sword.

"With a sturdy stick, I could walk." His belligerent gaze challenged Ronan.

Britta could not restrain herself. She looked at her father. "Can't you see? It's the best solution. This way we do not have to take his life, thus incurring the wrath of his formidable crew. He can return to his men and sail before we have to battle the Normans."

While it tore at her heart to think of an abrupt departure for Ari, she knew it was the only way he could be safe. The longer he stayed with them, the more suspicious Father and Ronan would grow of his motives. If he left now, he had a better chance of surviving this misguided venture into Ireland.

Ari shook his head, placing his hand over hers. "You do not understand. I will order my men to sail, but I will stay. There is no one better to face the Normans than a Viking. I know how they fight. I am weak, but I can help you." He bent at the waist in a half bow before addressing her father. "It is an honor to clear my name by fighting for you, King O'Shea."

CHAPTER 9

The king took his daughter's arm, walking her from Ari's room. Ronan trailed behind them, shooting the Viking a displeased glance. Ari caught a glimpse of two guards moving into position outside his door. They were taking no chances, now that they knew he could walk again. He recognized the burly guard he'd taken with him down the stairs, and the man gave him a murderous glare before the door latched.

After a short time, Florie brought him a meal, along with the surprising news that he was to attend the feast tonight. Did this mean the king would allow him to fight alongside his warriors? Perhaps he wanted to introduce them?

Or perhaps he planned to announce his death sentence.

He wished he could see out the high window to take his mind elsewhere, or that he had a book to look at. He missed those early days of Britta's unswerving attention, when she read to him for hours. Now he wasn't sure how she felt about him. She had suggested it was time for him to sail with his crew, so perhaps she wanted to be done with him.

He couldn't blame her.

He slurped down the hearty pea soup the nursemaid had brought then tore into a piece of dry bread to sop up the remainder. Were his men eating well? Had they been able to hunt? At the very least, they would have fish from the inlet and dried meat from their ships' supplies.

There was a soft rap at the door, and the guard opened it. Britta entered, carrying a pale green silken tunic and trousers, along with his leather boots. He hastily wiped pea soup from his mouth and stood.

She smiled shyly. "These clothes are for the feast. We had to borrow them from Clancy, since he is the only one your size, and the trousers may still be short. He was none too happy about it. Since there is no one with feet as large as yours, you must wear your own boots, though the servants could not clean all the dirt off."

He felt an actual blush creeping up his cheeks. Did she find his large feet repulsive? Taking the clothing and boots, he remained mute, unsure how to ask the question driving him mad. Would he live or die? Surely she knew.

She spoke up. "I know you are anxious. Please know that my father is a fair king. He does not make decisions carelessly."

"I am sure Ronan has said much against me." He couldn't keep the spite from his tone. He knew Ronan's concern for this castle went deeper than loyalty to the king. The looks the Irishman gave Britta only confirmed that he cared for her deeply.

Her eyebrows crinkled. "You assume much."

"I assume only that he is not blind to the beauty living under the same roof and that he might want her for himself." He gave her a pointed look.

Now it was Britta's turn to blush.

✦

"God will work things together for good." Britta managed to blurt the verse out before leaving Ari's room, unable to tamp down the fire in her cheeks. The Viking had no understanding of her God, so why had she felt compelled to say it?

She prayed Father would accept Ari's offer to serve with his soldiers, but it was impossible to know what his decision would be. This morning, she had told him that she believed Ari's intent was good, yet she did not say anything beyond that. If she pleaded for the Viking's life, it might make the king suspicious of her motives and give him further cause to eliminate Ari, or at least to expel him from their shores.

Instead, she put on her walking boots, told Florie she was going outside, and passed through the back door into the garden. Fruit trees had begun to blossom, and the heavy scent of their white petals filled the air. Honeybees from their hive box swarmed the holly bushes, humming past her ears. A bold squirrel chirruped at her from its perch on the rock wall.

How restorative spring was! And how fine to walk the pleasant land she would one day call her own.

Unless…

Unless Father demanded Ari's execution tonight at the feast. It was not hard to imagine Ronan, standing with his sword at the long table, prepared to fulfill such a command. No one would intervene. She imagined Ari's strong jaw dropping to his chest as his head slumped over, his powerful arms going limp as the blade cut into him.

She sank into the soft moss. Of course she would never allow that to happen, even if it meant throwing away any inheritance her father would leave her. The Viking wanted to learn—she saw it in his eyes as she read the Latin books to him. He was an adventurer at heart, like she was, although her adventures thus far had only been in her mind.

All these years, she had felt the draw of the unknown, even as she dreaded meeting it. Perhaps God was using this Viking to push her from her cozy nest. Perhaps she would need to free Ari then steal off with him as he sailed to his homeland.

She smiled at the image. Britta O'Shea, book-loving castle dweller, willingly joining a crew of Vikings. How absurd. She shook her head.

Florie stepped into the herb garden, cutting shears and basket at the ready. Snipping off a few sprigs of rosemary, she spoke aloud. "You're lost in thought, Princess. Anything you want to talk about?"

The woman was always sensitive to her moods.

"I don't know what God wants me to do with my life, Florie."

"What do you want to do with it?"

Britta laughed. "What does it matter what I want? God seems to want great sacrifice. Think of how brave Moses had to be, or the prophets. Think of our own Patrick, away from his home. Perhaps I must leave my home to find my future."

Florie gave her a thoughtful look. "Sometimes the greatest sacrifice is the one that takes you unawares. I had my own dreams of leaving this land, of returning to my home in England. But James became ill, and I don't regret staying here all these years—for him, and for *you*." She patted Britta's cheek then tucked several leaves of basil into her basket before leaving the garden.

❖

FATHER GREETED her with a kiss as she came into the great hall in the late afternoon. She hoped this was a sign that he had listened to her request to have mercy on Ari.

"You are the most beautiful princess in Ireland, my Britta. Fresh as a white rose."

She spun in the pale blue velvet dress he had brought her, enjoying the swirl of its flared skirt. Buttons ran in a straight line down the bodice, skirt, and wide sleeves, and dark blue satin trimmed the hem. She fingered the pearl crown on her head, hoping the twists of hair Florie had secured beneath it would not come loose and give her a bedraggled appearance.

Ronan positioned himself next to Father, his familiar red tunic draped with gold fabric. He could easily be mistaken for the king himself, even without a crown. He raised his dark eyebrows at Britta, and she detected only one well-hidden emotion in the depths of his eyes: sadness.

Had he and Father decided to execute Ari? Or was he upset because she cared for the welfare of a barbarian?

Her father's men were situated around the table, eating cheese and bread until the main course was brought out. The pleasantly heavy smells of herbed pork and stuffed pheasant filled the hall, stirring her hunger. She looked up at the dark oil portraits hung over the hearth, boasting generations of O'Sheas. Would her portrait and her children's portraits hang there someday? Or would the castle fall to the Normans first?

A hush fell over the room as the guards opened the door and Ari made his way toward the table. He clung to a wooden staff, yet his steps were more sure than she had expected. Even struggling to stand, his presence dominated the room. The pale green of the tunic seemed to cast a glow on his fair hair and beard, making him look almost angelic.

She wanted to stand and shout, "How could you ever take this man's life?" But she held her tongue, reminding herself this beautiful foreigner had tried to attack their castle. She would wait for her father's judgment.

After prayer, Father began to speak before the heaping dishes were passed. "You men know by now that this Viking, Ari, has offered to join our forces against the Normans. He regrets his hasty and misguided attempt to capture our castle, and he plans to tell his own crew to set sail without him. We have spent much time and prayer seeking fairness in this matter —for our people and for the Viking."

Britta looked into her father's gray eyes, praying for the right decision. If he chose to sentence Ari to death, she would be forced to act. Her heart would not allow her otherwise. She would have to steal into Ari's room, release him, and leave her treasonous shame behind and sail with him.

If he would let her.

CHAPTER 10

Ari could not tear his eyes from Britta's anxious gaze. The appetizing smell of food only reminded him that this might be his last meal.

King O'Shea's voice echoed in the hall. "We have decided that we need Ari to help us fight the Normans. He can tell us of their weapons and train us to defeat them. We cannot let our kingdom fall, as King Tynan's did. We must stop the Normans here."

The soldiers looked to Ronan for his agreement, and the man slowly nodded. "It is the best way."

Britta clamped a fist to her mouth, eyes wide, as if repressing a cry. Ari fought the urge to rush around the table to her side.

"I will speak to my men this day," Ari said. "I am indebted to you and your people."

"Thank you, Father—and Ronan," Britta breathed.

Ari watched as the mighty Irishman rested a tender gaze on the princess. He did not speak a word, but it was clear Ronan had only spared his life for Britta's sake.

FLORIE HAD FIRMLY INSTRUCTED Ari to strengthen his weak foot by walking, so he changed clothes after the feast and hobbled out into the fading sunlight. A lone guard sat by the door, engrossed in eating a small pie.

Ari was thankful his bruises had begun to fade, and perhaps this brief activity would strengthen his foot still more, so he would not appear quite so shocking when he saw his men. He wondered if Sigfrid watched the castle, even now. Or perhaps he had stayed at the camp, honoring Britta's truce.

Lost in thought, Ari stumbled over a stray limb and his foot gave out. A gasp sounded from a tree above as his knees thudded to the ground.

He looked up into the drift of white blossoms that covered a gnarled apple tree. He could barely make out one black leather shoe that protruded from under a yellow skirt.

"I'm coming." Britta's voice sounded from her perch on a higher limb. She skillfully wove between the branches, keeping her skirts tucked as she descended. She carefully deposited a heavy book on the ground before dropping to her feet.

The guard grunted and looked up, but when Britta shook her head, he went back to his pie.

She braced her feet and grasped Ari's hands in an attempt to pull him up. Knowing she couldn't possibly bear his weight with her small frame, he used his good foot to thrust himself upward. As he returned to a standing position, she noted his labored breathing and gave him a half smile.

"I am afraid I was of little use to you." She handed him the walking stick.

"You tried to aid me. I do not deserve your kindness."

She led the way toward a wooden bench that was surrounded by silvery mounds of lavender. Silence settled as they lowered onto it, but it was not uncomfortable. He inhaled the honeyed Irish scents of spring, which mingled with the fresh fragrance of Britta's thick black hair.

"My book!" She jumped up, racing to retrieve it from its grassy bed.

He laughed. "Why drag such a heavy book into a tree?"

She was surprisingly serious as she answered, her voice charged with emotion. "This book is one of my favorites. It tells the story of Patrick, a man who was taken from Britain and made an Irish slave, yet he later returned to Ireland to share the truth about God."

"And you...admire this man?"

She looked over the gardens, unable to meet his eyes. "Like him, I have always wanted to tell others about God."

A quiet nudge moved him to say, "Perhaps you could tell me. Our gods have done nothing for me."

Tentatively, she shared the story of Jesus Christ with him. As she did, the voice he'd heard in the darkest recesses of his soul seemed to grow stronger, almost humming in anticipation. This God she spoke of had sacrificed His own Son for humans, so they could join forces with Him on earth then live with Him forever in His kingdom.

Her eyes shone as she spoke of how she could cry to Him in the depths of the night, knowing He would hear.

"When my mother died, all I had was Florie and my books. My father was often too engrossed in his royal duties to spend time with me. I began to read the scriptures then, and somehow my eyes were opened."

A sudden longing possessed him—he wanted to read. He wanted to know for himself what treasures her holy book held.

His hand fell to the bench, unwittingly covering hers. Instead of moving his hand like he should, he wrapped his fingers around hers, savoring the velvety feel of her skin.

Fighting the urge to bring her hand to his lips, he met her dark blue eyes. "Teach me to read, Britta."

She smiled, and he had to focus on the apple tree to resist the pull of her innocent, upturned face. "I will. But only if you teach me your language."

✦

BRITTA WATCHED from the castle gate as Ronan and Ari rode on horseback toward the Viking encampment in early-evening light. Ronan had demanded to ride alongside the Viking, to be certain he did not try to break his promise and escape with his crew.

She watched Ari's movements carefully. His bad foot hung a bit too limply from the stirrup on their gray stallion, but he did not slump, so his stomach bruising must be healing.

Looking at the dirt road leading toward King Tynan's kingdom, she shuddered, imagining fully armed Normans charging toward the castle. They would probably wear steel helmets and chain mail. Perhaps they would laugh when they saw the size of her father's castle. How simple to take such a meager outpost!

Florie came alongside her, taking off her kerchief and smoothing her skirts. She was going home, goodies from the feast tucked into a basket at her side. Another townswoman would set out their food late in the evening, since there were many things left over from the grandiose banquet.

"Watching your Viking, are you?" Florie winked.

"What? I don't understand your meaning."

"Don't think I didn't see the two of you in the garden earlier, talking thick as thieves. Why, I even heard your father asking Ronan about your interest."

Britta snorted. Florie had likely been listening outside her father's chamber last night while the men talked. Her nursemaid believed it was her duty to stay abreast of all the affairs of the castle, on the pretense the princess needed to stay aware of such things.

Ronan. The man had listened to her, protected her, even stood up to her father on her behalf, for as long as she could recall. And now she returned his unspoken affection with open interest in a complete stranger's life.

Florie patted her hand. " 'Tis naught you can do, m'lady. The heart will answer when it is called. No flood, no earthquake, no falling stars can stop it. I see how you look at him, how you cling to his every word. Ronan loves you, 'tis sure, but you've given him no promises."

It was true. "Thank you. Tell James I will visit him tomorrow to borrow his new book."

Florie huffed. "He paid out the nose for that trifle, I tell you. But the man loves nothing more than reading. Takes him away from his pains, he says."

How well did she understand that. In fact, she'd taught James to read to offer some reprieve from his suffering. They had fallen into the habit of trading books so they could discuss their merits and inconsistencies. James had a simplistic way of looking at the world—and he would often miss nuances in the writing—but he had a way of perceiving overarching themes that took Britta's breath away.

Would she ever have such intense discussions with Ari? Although he seemed the type who was a born warrior and leader, he also had a natural candor and seemed to delight in learning.

Florie hugged her briefly and set off toward her home, skirts kicking up dust.

Britta stared at the field that led to the encampment. If only she could have joined the men, but neither of them would have allowed it.

Ronan knew that if Ari turned on him, one word from the Viking leader would mean his death. She had to believe that Ronan saw some measure of trustworthiness in Ari, perhaps because of his willingness to stay behind and fight for them.

Regardless, she began to pray.

CHAPTER 11

As the Viking camp finally came into view, Ari exhaled. His friends—his people—watched as they approached. He took in the familiar earthy smells of camp. How he longed to join his men on their return voyage, to see his parents again. But he brought no news of a vengeful victory for his brother's death. Instead, he must now fight to protect the very people he had hated for so long.

Sigfrid strode over, his eye appraising Ari's injured foot, his foreign clothing, and the Irishman astride the large white mare.

He spoke rapidly in Norse. "What has occurred? Should we kill this man?"

Ari shook his head, motioning for the men to help him down. He groaned when his injured foot touched the ground, and his crew was visibly dismayed as he pulled the walking staff from his saddle so he could stand.

Sigfrid repeated, "What has occurred?"

Ari spoke loudly, so all could hear. "Many things, but the most important is this: I led you to the wrong castle. This family has done nothing to my brother. They are innocent of his blood."

Unbridled chatter broke out among the men, and Sigfrid commanded silence. At his shout, Ronan's dark gaze turned sharp and his hand dropped to his sword.

Sigfrid shot Ronan a glare then motioned to Ari's foot. His lips tightened and his jaw flexed. "But they have injured you."

"No. This was my own doing. It is too much to explain. You must believe that they have carefully nursed my wounds."

Sigfrid glanced at Ronan, looking doubtful. He suspected the Irishman had forced him to say this.

"You saw their princess," Ari added. "She is incapable of harming someone."

At this, Sigfrid finally relaxed. Britta had made an impression. He slapped Ari's shoulder, excited. "We shall sail tomorrow, then. The longships are ready, and it will not take long to pack up camp."

The men whooped for joy, but Ari held up his hand. "*You* may surely sail tomorrow. But I have promised to aid this kingdom as the Normans will soon descend upon it. I must do this for my family honor, which was marred when I brought us here."

Sigfrid leaned in uncomfortably close, gripping Ari's cheeks in his dirty hand, his heavy breath on his face. Ari squirmed under the relentless gaze. He should have known he could not fool his old friend and battle partner.

"You want the girl!" Sigfrid finally declared, giving him a crooked smile. "This is not only about honor. I knew your heart was searching when we set sail, and now you've found the treasure you really sought."

The men had fallen silent, and Ronan shifted uncomfortably in his saddle, poised to gallop away if the men turned on him.

Ari decided to put his mind at ease. He spoke to the Irishman in his own language. "They understand."

Some of the fire went out of Ronan's eyes, but his expression remained wary.

Ari spoke to his men. "You will sail tomorrow. I will find another way back after I battle the Normans. There will be no plunder for you here."

The men murmured in agreement. They began to thump him on the back, saying their good-byes.

As the crew dispersed, Ari pulled Sigfrid into a hug and whispered into his ear, "Tell my parents of what has happened. Someday, I will find a way home."

The grizzled man nodded, but his eye glistened. He surely knew Ari's promise was in vain. This was likely their final farewell.

Burying his sadness, Ari turned toward Ronan. "It is settled. Now we return to the castle."

As the horses trotted off, he took one last glance at the men who had followed him so loyally. The Irish soldiers would never respect him as these men had—in fact, they probably despised him for breaking their man's arm. They would doubtless relegate him to the rear flank, given his foot injuries.

Yet it was no one's fault but his own. His bitterness and grief had culminated in this disgrace.

He would make amends the only way he knew how. He would lay down his hatred of the Irish, even as he laid down his life.

◆

BEHIND THEM, the sun had nearly sunk into the horizon. The horses plodded on, anxious for fresh hay. When they were a good distance away from the camp, Ronan finally spoke.

"Why are you really joining us?"

Ari remained silent, letting his thoughts slide into order. Truly, he was motivated by the desire to restore his family honor. He had no wish to stoke the fires of fear and hatred the

Irish rightly felt toward the Northmen, due to raids that had occurred centuries ago.

Yet Sigfrid had discerned a deeper need that had led him to these distant shores. The need for answers to his unasked questions. Why had Egil died so young? What was the point of living if he didn't strive for the gods' favor? What hope was there for him if he doubted the existence of Valhalla? At home in Norway, he had suspected the Christian churches held answers, but he did not want to openly defy his parents' beliefs to attend.

Now he was in Ireland, at the wrong castle, and a princess had begun to tell him of the same Christian God he sought.

Ronan did not prod him, but he finally answered. "I must atone for my foolhardiness."

"There is another reason," Ronan said firmly. He gave him a stormy gaze that said he was unwilling to accept half-truths.

"It is true, I find Princess Britta very endearing. But I understand there is no hope for us. Her father would never let her marry a Northman."

"So you have thought of marriage." Although Ronan's tone was careless, Ari sensed calculation.

"I have," he admitted, as much to himself as to Ronan. "But I understand she is betrothed to you."

Ronan's expression soured. "There is no such betrothal."

The Irishman could have lied outright to protect his interest in Britta. Instead, he had told Ari the truth.

Ari took a long look at the glowering man riding by his side. He seemed to be in pain. Was his love for Britta so great?

The castle came into view, putting an end to his musing. Now was the time to prepare for battle, not to discuss the princess. Ronan seemed to understand the shift of focus and urged his horse into a trot.

Britta walked out to greet them, carrying Ari's sheathed

sword. Her smile of relief was quickly replaced with a serious look. After he dismounted, she handed Peacebreaker to him. "Father says you must begin training immediately. The men are gathered in the courtyard. The Normans have been sighted, only a couple days' journey from us."

CHAPTER 12

Training began straightaway, even in the gathering darkness. Britta insisted on aiding the townswomen by keeping torches lit and giving the men water.

Ronan had demanded that the handful of men who had chain mail wear it when sparring, so even in the cool of the evening, they overheated easily. Britta made sure the water bucket stayed full so they could occasionally wipe down with wet cloths, a luxury they would not have in battle.

After serving the men, she retreated up to her stone balcony, where she could get a better view of the clashing swords, shields, maces, and daggers. Some of the men wore bull-hide vests that would scarce protect them from the well-armed Normans. Some had no protection at all.

She felt grieved by the poorly dressed state of her father's soldiers, but most Irish kingdoms were the same. If only they were wealthier, able to afford well-crafted swords like Ari's. She had caught Ronan coveting that shiny blade, touching it to see how sharp it was.

Ari's family must be wealthy. Perhaps his father was a chieftain or king? She cringed, knowing the Viking royals probably rose to power with the aid of plunder they took from Irish monasteries.

The courtyard training was halted by a deep shout from Ari. He stood, one hand in the air, as if to silence everyone. Was he unable to spar with his injured foot?

Even as Ronan strode toward him, Ari began to guide the scattered Irish soldiers into a formation. He barked a word here or there to indicate what they were to do—some were to move forward with shields while others protected the sides with swords and maces. The men with daggers were sent away, only to return bearing spears.

From what Father and Ronan had told her, the Irish soldiers rarely used a structured formation in battle. They placed a high value on surprising their enemies, rather than meeting them head-on. Most of her father's soldiers were simply landowners and slaves; they understood more of farming than of fighting. Thus far, the only invaders they had faced were loose marauding groups from other kingdoms, bent on stealing cattle.

To be safe, her father had already ordered the women, children, and elderly to take the cattle and livestock into the caves of Crow Mountain. Although it would be slow travel at night, they would be out of harm's way by morning.

Father had recommended she accompany the group to the mountain, but at Ronan's insistence, he had allowed Britta to make the final decision. She wanted to be close to Father, no matter what happened, so she planned to stay with James and Florie in their cottage during the attack. It was doubtful any Norman would trail to the outskirts of the village, much less care about raiding a small farmhouse.

Her attention was pulled back to the sparring men below. Ronan and Ari stood off in a mock battle, but their intense, savage looks made her catch her breath. Ari held his gleaming sword and shield, and Ronan held his beloved mace and smaller shield. As the weapons clashed in a slow, deliberate fashion, it became obvious that although Ari still favored his injured foot, her father's toughest warrior would be bested by the Viking.

At the last moment, however, Ronan dealt a feigned, final blow that knocked Ari's sword to the ground. Both men nodded briefly out of respect then began to practice with the next man in line.

Would they be able to prepare her father's men in time? Would they know how to defeat the Normans?

As Ari effortlessly knocked an unprepared, helmeted man to the ground with his shield, she began to doubt it.

◆

ARI HAD HOPED the second day of sparring would be easier than the first, but it had proved more difficult. The men were tired from fighting yesterday and from doing farm chores in the morning. They hadn't had enough sleep to build up their energy.

But war never came at a convenient time. And these Irishmen had to understand how to counter the Norman attack.

If only he had one of his father's berserkers with him. Just one of those wild warriors could stave off many men and strike fear into the rest.

Sigfrid and the men would be under full sail by now. Longship voyages were always indescribably fulfilling experiences. He could almost feel the rush of sea air against his skin—that briny, fresh smell that made him feel so alive. How he loved pulling the oars those final lengths as they glided into the fjords of home. The deep blue sky and the formidable mountains always seemed to rein them in with invisible hands.

As Britta brought a loaf of bread to the table, he wished he could share his thoughts with her. Maybe she would someday sail with him and enjoy the delights of the sea, but if he could not stop the Normans, his death would be sure.

He did have one question to ask her before he fought, however. He withdrew his bronze bottle from his tunic and set it on the table.

"Around the neck of this bottle, there are letters. I wondered if you could tell me what they say?"

She traced each letter of the inscription with her finger. Some were worn, and he wondered if she could make them out. But it did not take long for a smile to break across her face.

"Spero." She carefully returned the bottle to his open palm. "It is a Latin word, probably carved by monks." Sadness briefly replaced her joy. "You have stolen this from the Irish monks?"

"Not I. But yes, my family did, generations ago." He could not restrain his curiosity. "What does it mean?"

She took a deep breath, a shiver running up her arms. "Perhaps it is a sign—a whisper from God. The word means *hope.*"

He started. It was the very word he had heard so clearly in his spirit. Did it mean there was hope for him with Britta? Hope the Irish would triumph?

Or did it mean he had hope of salvation by the Christian God?

"There is always hope," she murmured, catching his gaze. "I have spent too much time fearing the worst. But God will watch over His own, even if it means carrying us home to heaven."

"I will not let that happen to you." He took her hand, toying with her large amber ring. Perhaps someday he could give her a ring of his own.

Ronan stood abruptly, motioning the men back to the courtyard. As Ari rose to join them, he handed the bottle back to Britta. "Keep this safe for me. I will retrieve it after the battle."

Tears sprang into her eyes, but she cradled the bottle in her hands. "I am honored to do so."

He continued. "And to keep the bottle safe, you must promise me you will stay hidden, no matter what happens."

"I promise." Her voice wavered, and he had to fight the urge to pull her into his arms.

This was no time to go soft because of a woman. He strapped on his sword. He would channel the heat and fire of his emotions into sheer rage against the invading Normans. He would put thoughts of Britta, with her soft hands and heart, out of his mind for now.

CHAPTER 13

Father joined Britta on the balcony to watch the warriors. She tried to read the thoughts behind his serious gray gaze but could not.

When the grunts and shouts lulled, he spoke. "I understand your desire to stay with Florie and James. But I have not been able to sleep, knowing the risks of that dangerous choice. It is too late for you to follow the others to the mountain, but you must allow me to set a guard outside their house."

She did not want to go against her father, but at the same time, she knew every warrior was needed for the battle to come. Although her father's men seemed to have improved in technique, their number was still abysmal. It would not require many Normans to overtake them, especially if they were on horseback.

Father gave her no time to respectfully decline. Instead, he patted her cheek, as if she were still a young child, and peered into her face.

"Britta, I must ask you. Have you any interest in Ronan?"

"Not as a husband." The speed and certainty of her response surprised her.

"Yet you know him so well, and you have been friends these many years." He shifted in his seat, adjusting the golden belt wrapped around his linen tunic. He looked at the heavy purple clouds that hovered above them. "I knew how he felt toward you, of course. But I implored him to approach you only as a friend and mentor. In fact, I do believe I threatened to banish him from the kingdom should he be bold with his feelings toward you."

So that was why Ronan had never declared his love! No wonder he had never discussed his heart with her. There had been too much at stake.

Father continued. "But now you are of marriageable age, and I must acknowledge there are many who seek to wed my beautiful daughter. I thought perhaps you had developed feelings for Ronan of your own accord, without his prodding."

As if summoned by their conversation, Ronan charged through the doorway. Removing his helmet, he ran a hand through his sweaty hair, making the front of it stand up straight. He unsheathed his sword.

Father jumped to his feet. "What is the meaning—"

"No time to talk," Ronan breathed. "I am taking Britta."

She stepped back, gripping the ledge of the balcony so she wouldn't topple to the ground below. "What are you about, Ronan?"

He dropped into a curt bow, his dark eyes apologetic. "I must rush you to Florie's home. Norman troops have been spotted on horseback, just outside our western wood." He turned to her father. "King O'Shea, Ari will guard you until I return. The men are preparing their weapons and armor, and Clancy is gathering our horses."

Ari stepped onto the balcony behind Ronan. His blue eyes were cold, like the frozen waterfalls she marveled at in winter. His jaw clenched, and his cheekbones formed angular lines. For a fleeting moment, she saw the deadly Viking who had fearlessly invaded their castle, and he was a terrifying sight—a Norwegian giant with no aim but to conquer his foe.

Ari pressed a hand on Father's back, leading him into the castle. Impulsively, Britta strode over to hug her father. He gave her a sad smile, kissed her forehead, and said, "Promise you will stay safe. You are my only heritage, my most valued treasure."

She nodded, and Ronan loosely wrapped his fingers around her upper arm. His sword remained in his other hand, ready to carve a path, should the need arise. She met his searching gaze. Did he hope for a declaration of love in these final moments of uncertainty?

"Come," he said gently, pulling her from the balcony. "You cannot be seen here. And leave the crown behind."

She had forgotten she was wearing her small jeweled crown today. Florie had instructed her to do so, to cheer the men as they fought for her and for their kingdom. She removed it, shoving it into a bookshelf as they left the room. She turned, remembering Ari's bottle on the balcony, but it was too late to retrieve it.

As they passed through the kitchen, she snatched Florie's long linen shawl and draped it around her silk dress, hoping to further conceal her royalty.

Ronan nodded at the wisdom of her action and then pointed to her long, flowing hair. She quickly knotted it as the commoners did. As they entered the back garden, she took a handful of dirt and smeared it on her face and hands.

"You are stronger than you think," Ronan observed.

The simple words made tears spring into her eyes. It was what she had always loved about Ronan—he believed in her, and he always spoke the truth.

"Will Father fight?" She could barely ask. If only Ari were whisking him into hiding, just as Ronan was hiding her.

"He must fight. This is no time for hiding in the shadows. Your father is a skilled warrior, and his presence will inspire the men to greater sacrifice." Ronan slowed, taking in her face, which seemed to be frozen in terror. Although he gripped her hand, it still felt chilled.

He rubbed her hand with his battle-toughened fingers. "You are going to live, Britta. James and Florie will protect you. Your father will also live—you can be sure I will let no harm come to him."

She felt like bursting into tears, knowing Ronan would definitely lay down his life for her father's, but she nodded briefly and scrambled over the nearby stone wall. She would not detain this warrior any longer than necessary.

"Thank you," she said, knowing he caught every undercurrent of anxiety and sadness in her words.

"You are my princess," he replied.

✦

AFTER CROSSING several fields and pastures, they arrived at James and Florie's humble farmhouse. Britta tried not to think of the numerous cow piles she hadn't been able to avoid, but she knew her cloth shoes were utterly ruined.

Ronan gave five sharp raps on Florie's short wooden door, and the woman hastened to open it. Britta could make out nothing inside the hut, and she realized curtains had been pulled over the windows, plunging it into a deliberate darkness.

James spoke up from his bed. "We been waitin' on you, Princess. And prayin.'"

She stepped over the stone threshold, turning to catch one last glimpse of Ronan. He nodded at her, a strange shaft of sunlight piercing the heavy clouds and lighting his dark hair. With his sword in hand and a fierce look on his face, he looked ready to single-handedly take on the Norman armies.

"Bolt the door behind me. If anyone comes and does not

knock five times, do not open the door. Florie, do you have a weapon?"

Her nursemaid nodded. "Aye, we have a spear and James's sword. I will give Britta my dagger."

"It will do." Ronan looked directly at Britta's face. "Stay hidden. And if you are found out, keep the dagger close. We do not know how the Normans treat their conquests..."

As his voice trailed off, she grasped his unspoken thought. Perhaps it would be better to kill herself than to be taken by the invaders.

"I understand," she whispered.

Florie hugged her. "Now, off with you, m'lord. We have everything in hand."

Ronan gave a short bow and left for the castle without another word.

As Florie bolted the door, Britta walked to James's bedside. She could hardly make out his face, but he took her hand in his. "Now you must be strong, m'lady. You must hide in the kitchen cupboard. It's dark and tight, and Florie will pack sacks of wheat and dried meats around you, so it might not smell the best. But I swear to you, they won't live to find you."

The certainty in his tone verified his words. Her sickly friend would doubtless stagger from his bed to protect her. And she shuddered to think of what her beloved nursemaid would do before she let anyone approach her princess.

"Thank you," she repeated, the inadequacy of the words squeezing at her heart like hot blacksmith's tongs. Would they live to see tomorrow? Would she ever be able to thank her loyal friends for their willingness to sacrifice their lives?

Would God let the O'Shea kingdom stand?

CHAPTER 14

After helping the king into his battle attire, Ari paced outside the room. Ronan was taking a long time returning. Did it mean he had been waylaid? Surely he had kept to the back paths.

Ronan had told him not to assemble the troops until his arrival, but what if that did not happen? Ari had to do something—they couldn't be caught unawares. He approached the king's door and knocked.

"Enter."

Ari bowed his head as he stepped through the shorter chamber door, an unintended reminder of his lowly position here. He should be leading the troops, giving orders, yet he had to place himself under the king and Ronan.

"I believe it is time to move into position," he said.

The king turned toward his window, watching his men as they milled around the courtyard, full of restless energy. "I agree."

It did not take long to muster the men. Ari cringed again when his gaze traveled over the unimpressive force. Without

Ronan's strength and experience, he and the king would likely be the most skilled warriors.

But the king had not practiced with them, presumably to save his energy. Ari suspected he was weary from his recent extended trek across the countryside. King O'Shea was not a young man anymore. Some older men, like Sigfrid, were strong warriors, but they had to train their bodies every day for the fight.

Perhaps this was Ari's chance to step up and lead the Irishmen. But he feared he would lead them to defeat instead of victory, given his lingering injury.

Britta's forlorn parting look filled his memory. She would be crushed if her father died and the castle fell to the Normans. Even worse, she might be abused at the hands of the bold invaders.

Fresh vigor filled his veins, a protective rage he had not felt since the day his brother returned to their longship, bloody and gasping for life. He would never let them touch her. She was so trusting, so compassionate. Perhaps her faith in the one God would be sufficient, but Ari would do anything to aid her God in keeping her safe.

Clomping hooves pounded the dirt and one of their spotters raced up the road, his stallion frothing at the mouth. The sentry attempted to speak several times, but words would not come forth. Finally, he gave a hoarse shout.

"Prepare! They are nearly upon us!"

Ari led the men as they surged forward, limping only a little. He refused to ride a horse, to show the men he would not seek to escape if the battle did not go in their favor.

Using rocks, ditches, and the trees lining the road, he pointed select men to their hiding places. They would try to use the terrain to their advantage.

The chains groaned and shook as the castle gate was drawn up behind them. The horsemen pulled up the rear line near the gate, both to keep the animals alive as long as possible and to give them a powerful advantage, should the initial attack come to naught.

The king produced a bright yellow sash for Ari to drape over his chain mail. "The men must be able to locate you quickly," he explained. Ari knew Ronan's red tunic was the one the men were accustomed to. He tried not to ponder what sort of person could have stopped the Irish warrior in his race to join the troops.

"Will you speak to your men now?" Ari asked.

King O'Shea shook his head. "You must rally them. You will be their commander in this battle. I must needs saddle my horse and take up my position by the castle door."

Ari nodded, accepting the task that had fallen to him in Ronan's absence. He climbed onto a nearby rock, ignoring a slight twinge in his bruised foot. At least he was able to keep his balance without his stick now. His words filled the air, silencing the men.

"Look here. I am not one of you, but I wholeheartedly fight for you. Call it fate, call it God, call it what you will, but I am here and I will not retreat. Hear me now: I will *never* retreat. We will win this battle and grind those half-breed Normans into the dirt. Not a one of them will live to tell others of their hideous defeat. Fight for your king, fight for your land, and fight for your honor!"

The men beat their shields in a slow rhythm, shouting their enthusiasm. As the Norman horses topped the first hill, the chants of the Irishmen roared in a wild cacophony.

Before the first arrow flew, Ronan shoved his way through the ranks, sword and shield at the ready. He took his place next to Ari. His voice rumbled out, full of determination and a deeper sentiment.

"For Britta."

Ari nodded, drawing his shield close. "For Britta."

MOMENTS FADED into hours as Britta lay on her side in the pitch-dark cupboard. Sounds were muffled by the food sacks that had been closely pressed around her. Florie had not shirked in making sure the Normans would never suspect that someone could fit into the space she now occupied. If she ever emerged, she would smell like garlic cloves, and it might take days to comb the spilled grains out of her hair.

Was it day or night? Florie would not open the door to speak to her, for fear the Normans would burst inside that very moment. Before Britta had clambered into her hiding space, both Florie and James had given her a final hug and sworn again to protect her at all costs.

As a distraction from her tight, stuffy quarters, she let her mind roam where it wanted. She touched her mother's ring. Had Mother ever faced an invasion of this size? If so, did she run and hide, or sit proudly on her throne? Britta hated that she didn't know the answer to these questions. All Father had ever spoken of was her mother's beauty, but surely there had been more depth to her character?

And Ronan. The man was a wall of support to her, a friend from her childhood who had never failed to treat her with respect. A beautiful Irishman, truth be told, with his flashing eyes and dark hair. A man among men. He felt strongly for her, she knew. But was it the kind of love she wanted from a husband?

She couldn't stop herself as her thoughts jumped to Ari. What pulled her to the towering Northman who had come to plunder their castle? Was it his honesty, his willingness to admit he had been wrong? Or was it that love of learning new languages and words, a love she shared?

A tingle ran through her, forcing her to acknowledge that on some level, her attraction was purely instinctual. Every time the man touched her arm or hand, her mind danced into some star-strewn realm where it seemed nothing could ever hurt her again.

Yet she knew such visions were unrealistic. Hadn't she seen James struggle to make ends meet for his farm after he was struck with the coughing disease? Hadn't she watched Florie cry for days when she feared James had taken a turn for the worse?

One thing she knew: real love was not easy. It was not floating on a cloud of happiness. Life and death, survival and failure, happiness and grief were woven together with the unbreakable cords of marriage.

She had to choose carefully which man she tied herself to.

CHAPTER 15

Things were not going well.

The Irish archers in the woods had initially caught the Normans by surprise, but it did not take long for the invaders to rally and gallop into their ranks, forcing them to scatter. Although the Irish warriors had managed to unhorse many Normans with their spears, they were at a disadvantage in hand-to-hand combat because the Normans were well outfitted with chain mail and helmets.

For each Norman Ari cut down with his sword, two Irishmen fell to the rocky ground they fought on. To make things worse, the heavy clouds finally burst into rain, making their leather shoes lose their grip on the uneven terrain.

As a helmeted Norman thrust his spear at him, Ari parried the blow with his shield. The deerskin-covered wood cracked, and he groaned. If his shield broke, he was doomed.

Ronan made his way to Ari's side, dodging the Norman's thrusts and driving the mace into the man's neck, dropping him to the ground. He turned and threw a bleak smile Ari's way, but not before a Norman stalked up behind him and thrust a sword into his shoulder. Ronan's mace dropped, and he sank to the ground, blood spilling freely from his wound.

Ari howled like a wolf and charged the Norman, bringing him down with little effort. Even as he took up Ronan's mace and attacked more Normans, from the corners of his eyes he saw how many Irishmen lay scattered around him.

They were overwhelmed. There was no hope. And now Ronan might die, because he had tried to protect him.

Suddenly, another howl met his ears, and he recognized it immediately.

Sigfrid.

His friend had come!

His hopes renewed, he charged afresh, bringing down two Normans with one blow. Viking warriors crested the hill. His entire crew had returned!

The leather-clad Vikings swarmed the Normans like an angry hive of bees. Sigfrid stood back-to-back with Ari and they cleaved their way through their enemies, dropping bodies in their wake. Driven by the bloodlust of war, Ari nearly forgot his foot was injured.

Thanks to his warriors, the Irish victory came swiftly. When the battle was over, Ari was shocked at the good-sized group of Irishmen left standing. King O'Shea himself was only bleeding slightly from a leg wound.

He scanned the bodies for Ronan, but to no avail. The king pointed to the edge of the wood, where someone had positioned the fallen warrior out of the way. Ronan writhed in pain, his left arm hanging useless as the blood continued to spill from his shoulder.

Ari moved as quickly as his foot would allow, dropping to his knees at Ronan's side. Sigfrid joined him, tearing off his tunic and pressing it to the wound.

"Don't stand there gaping," Ari shouted to the nearby soldiers. "His groans are a good sign! Fetch us a cot!"

When the men returned, they were able to roll Ronan onto the cot, although he cried in pain when his wounded torso was handled. Inside the castle, the men positioned him on the floor in the small chamber where Ari had been held.

Ari watched as his best healer, Valgerd, removed Ronan's mail shirt then stuffed the wound with cloth to stanch the flow.

"We need herbs," Valgerd said. "If they have yarrow, that might slow the bleeding. There are other things I could use, should they have them."

Positioning Sigfrid by Ronan's side, Ari led the healer to the herb beds.

His man pinched off a handful of leaves. Finally, he said, "This is good, but do they keep dried herbs?"

One woman would know where all the herbs were and would be able to aid his man. Her faithful care had good results, as he could attest from the way his nearly healed foot had performed in battle. Florie. And Florie watched over Britta. He had to retrieve them both.

Racing toward the stables, Ari said, "Do your best. I will bring you a woman who can help."

He dug his heels into the horse's flanks, finally acknowledging a possibility he could no longer ignore. What if the Normans had sent forces into the village and fields before they had attacked the castle? Would he even reach Britta in time?

✦

BRITTA YAWNED. Her legs cramped beneath her. She tried to straighten them, knowing they would merely bash into the corner of the cupboard again. The only way to ignore her confined situation was to give in to sleep.

Just as she dozed off, thuds reverberated in the wood

beneath her. What was it? She strained to listen for voices but heard nothing more than muffled movement.

She pressed closer to the cupboard wall. She prayed the Normans would not harm Florie or James, that they would not search the small farmhouse and discover her. The dagger lay beneath her. She would need to snatch it if they dragged her out.

She shuddered. Would she be forced to kill herself before the Normans could harm her? And how would she do it? Stab herself in the heart? Surely she would lose strength the moment the knife entered, so maybe it wouldn't work.

The cupboard door swung open, and a hand fumbled toward her. She was blinded by the light that poured in, but she managed to still her breath, even though she could not silence the pounding of her heart.

The hand shoved several bags aside then grasped at the bag on her head and yanked it down. She tried to shift out of reach, but the hand touched her face and a familiar voice poured through her soul like a healing balm.

"M'lady! Have you heard a thing I was sayin'? 'Tis the Viking come to retrieve you."

"Oh! Thanks be to God!" She crawled from her hiding place, much to the apparent amusement of the Norse giant, who quirked a half smile at her. His trousers were filthy, and his hair fell wildly about his shoulders.

James sat on his bed, beaming. "They've held the castle, Princess! The Normans won't try for it again, I'll wager."

Ari helped her to her feet, but worry creased his brow. "We paid a heavy price for our victory. In truth, I have mostly come for Florie. Her skills are needed. Ronan has suffered injury."

Britta gasped for air, unable to fill her lungs.

"Ronan?" she croaked. Her head felt like she was underwater.

Smoothly, Ari slid his arm around the curve of her waist, steering her toward a chair. "You must sit. This has been a shock." He turned to Florie. "You take the horse. There is no time to waste. I will walk the princess back when she is ready."

Florie nodded, taking a moment to kiss James before she hurried out the door.

Britta rubbed her head and looked at Ari through foggy eyes. She took another deep breath. Was this really happening, or had she fallen asleep? Perhaps she was still in the cupboard.

Ari knelt at her side, bringing her hand to his lips. The moment she felt the soft pressure of his kiss, the room sharpened. She knew what she had to do.

"We must go," she said.

James protested from his cozy corner, but Ari examined her face. "You are certain you can walk? Your legs must be weak after your long confinement."

"I *will* walk. Ronan cannot die without knowing of my gratitude, my..." She could not articulate the words, and the tears she'd been holding back flooded her eyes. She vainly swiped at them with her sleeve.

Ari hesitantly used his large thumb to wipe tears from her cheek, his serious gaze meeting hers. "First you must drink something to restore your strength. Then we will go."

CHAPTER 16

Even after a cup of tea, Britta's legs still felt like wobbling jelly. She stretched several times up to her tiptoes, jumped around a bit, and then finally tucked her arm in Ari's to be sure she wouldn't collapse along the way.

James reluctantly let her go, but not before he gave Ari a stern lecture on what was expected in terms of gentlemanly behavior when walking alone with a woman.

Once they were halfway through the low grass of a hay field, a heavy sigh finally escaped her lips.

Ari did not probe, but he quirked an eyebrow, willing to listen.

She tried to give voice to her thoughts. "I am stricken that Ronan is hurt. But I am in awe that God has spared our castle." She turned to him. "I am thankful you fought for us."

"Were it left to me, all would have been lost." Irritation filled his voice. "We were outnumbered and underarmed, as we feared we might be." He squeezed her arm tighter, as if trying to protect her from the horrors he had seen. "Your Ronan saved my life."

She fell silent. He was not "her" Ronan. But she sensed there was more to the story. "Speak on."

He paused to sweep his unmanageable hair back into its leather tie. Without thinking, she reached up to help him, gathering handfuls of his blond locks. He stilled as her finger brushed his beard.

His voice was low and husky when he replied. "My men came to our aid. Sigfrid—the one you spoke to—said they had sailed but a short distance and something told him to return. If not for them, nothing could have stopped the slaughter."

"God must have spoken to his heart," she mused. Grass tugged at her skirts, beckoning her to sit and rest her weary feet. Releasing Ari's arm, she plopped down in the field none too daintily. "I need to stop," she said.

The sound of hooves pounding near the forest's edge caught her attention. Ari had already spotted the horse and rider. He bent and snatched her up, tossing her easily over his shoulder. He ran toward a rock formation perched atop an ocean inlet at the edge of the field. Placing her carefully in a damp crevice, he drew his sword and turned.

The horseman had not veered from their trail, and even worse, he wore Norman armor. He was shouting, but she could not make out what he said.

Yet the moment he stretched a finger toward her, repeating the same word with increasing vehemence, she knew what he had come for.

He wanted to capture her.

As Ari inexplicably scrounged for something on the ground, she shrank back into the shadows of the rocks. Had the remaining Normans already taken her father? How else would he know to search for a princess?

As the dark horse closed upon them, Ari rammed a long stick into the ground. To avoid it, the Norman flew past her rocky shelter. The horse jerked to a halt, plunging its rider over the edge of the overhang.

She wished she couldn't hear the man's groans as he wallowed on the rocks below. Ari turned to her, clasping her hand and pulling her back to her feet.

"I must finish this." His voice rose above the bloodcurdling sounds.

She nodded mutely.

Ari found an area where he could safely descend. The Norman continued to scream. In fact, the screams grew louder. What was Ari doing to him? Did the Vikings torture people?

Suddenly, Ari topped the overhang, dragging the Norman behind him. With each bounce, the man hurled insults in his language. When they reached Britta, Ari deposited the writhing invader at her feet.

"I thought this straggler could return to his people and share his tale of the Viking force that guards this castle." He sneered down into the man's cringing face, shaking his fist for good measure.

"Clever thinking. Thank you." She looked hopefully at the wide-eyed horse. The terrors of this day had taken their toll. "Perhaps we could ride the horse? You could bind the Norman here, and we could send one of our men out to retrieve him later. We aren't far from the castle now—it's just through that wood."

Ari nodded, removing the belt from his tunic and lashing the man to the trunk of a scraggly tree that had managed to withstand the ocean's blasts. For good measure, he tore a piece of the Norman's tunic and stuffed it into his mouth, stifling his continued protests.

Task complete, he took the horse's face in his hands. The beast started, but when Ari whispered into its face, it seemed to calm.

Ari extended a rock-solid arm to boost her onto the large

animal. Instead of taking it, she turned to face him, taking in his dirty clothing, once-again loosened hair, and concerned eyes. His cheeks were reddened in the salty air and his lips had fallen open, revealing surprisingly white teeth.

Propriety vanished as she tipped up into his arms, meeting his lips. She had never kissed a man, but it required no training. Their kiss was as natural as the waves pounding behind them, as the robins singing in the trees.

He pulled back, his soft beard pressing into her cheek as he kissed it. Then he cupped her face in his hands, regret etching his features.

"James has instructed me what I am to do when walking alone with a woman, and this was not mentioned."

She laughed, and his eyes crinkled in response. He extended his arm again.

"We must not linger."

Of course. They had to return to Ronan—what if he were lying on his deathbed? How had he slipped her mind, even for a moment? What had possessed her to practically attack Ari?

The overwrought black horse munched grass nearby. Ari walked up to it, again talking in his low voice as he took the reins. But when it gave a sudden rear kick, he sighed.

"We will have to walk. It is not safe for you to ride him. Perhaps after a good watering and brushing, he might tame down."

She nodded, trying to keep up with Ari as he led the anxious horse to the stables. Even with his slight limp, she had to jog alongside, taking three steps to match just one of his.

When she was near him, the soft linen of his tunic brushed her hand in a gentle rhythm. He glanced down at her often, his gaze soft and unguarded. The truth began to stir and waken in her spirit. Her heart had already chosen who it wanted, and he was not the one her father would approve of.

ARI FELT LIKE A FOOL, his damp leather shoes causing him to stumble along the dirt road. But Britta seemed oblivious to his clumsiness, holding on to his arm as if she floated on a cloud.

What would happen if Ronan woke from his stupor? Would he regret that he had nearly sacrificed his life for a rogue Viking? And what if Ronan did not wake? Britta would never forgive him for costing her faithful friend's life.

Had Ronan ever been more than a friend to Britta? It seemed he had not, but the desire had been there, at least on his part. It was understandable. She was a woman who was easy to love. She delighted in small things, like books and flowers. She was loyal to her family and friends. She was even willing to crush her royal body into a small cupboard for hours, never demanding a softer hiding place.

Although she was not a trained warrior, she was as resourceful as any Viking woman, and that was saying a great deal.

He couldn't hide his smile, slowing his stride when he realized she was having difficulty matching his pace. She was so small, so vulnerable... He could not bear to think what the Norman warrior might have done to her. He had heard tales of how they broke their conquests' arms and legs then threw their limp bodies over cliffs.

Violence for violence's sake. He had known some older Vikings who lived like this, who had embraced the killing. But his father had given up raiding when his brother died. And now, Ari realized he had no stomach for raiding, either. It was senseless.

As they neared the castle, Sigfrid came to greet them. His eye wandered over the fractious horse, the disheveled princess, and finally met Ari's weary gaze. He mercifully refrained from asking questions, motioning for a servant boy to stable the horse.

Sigfrid led them into the great hall, where Ari's men had gathered around the table. "You should eat. We've cooked up some of the meat that their healing woman told us to use."

Britta tugged Ari's sleeve. "But Ronan? Ask him how he fares. And my father?"

Ari knew she would not rest until she had a report. All thoughts of the Norman attacker flew as he put her questions to Sigfrid then translated his friend's reply. "With the aid of our Valgerd and Florie, Ronan will live. They watch his arm carefully, to be sure it will not need to be removed."

Britta let out a small cry. She understood that an armless warrior would not be able to lead, although he could still fight.

Hoping to soften her distress, he continued. "Your father's leg injury has been wrapped and it will heal. The cut was not deep."

Relief washed over her features. She glanced at his men, who lunged for their food like bears preparing for hibernation. "You should eat with them. I cannot imagine how weary you are from the battle. I must go to Ronan first."

"Of course you must," he said.

But in his deepest, darkest thoughts, some corner of his heart wished that Ronan would have died from that blow.

CHAPTER 17

Ronan watched Britta's every move as she flitted about, adjusting his blankets and bringing him fresh tea. The Viking healer had steeped the smelly concoction, and although Ronan looked as if he might gag, he forced himself to swallow it.

"I suppose if they wanted to kill me, this would be an easy way to do it," he said darkly.

She drew up a stool, covering his cold hand with her own. "They mean us no harm, I am sure of it. Why else would they have returned to fight alongside our men?"

"Yes...I will admit Ari is a remarkable warrior. I suppose your father will place him in charge of his forces now."

The jealousy in his tone was palpable. "Ronan!" she scolded. "Do not think that way. Of course you will still be Father's commander."

"Not if I lose my arm." He would not meet her eyes.

She twined her fingers into his. "You will not. With the herbal ministrations of two skilled healers, your shoulder is healing quickly! Why, Florie only had to lightly stitch it."

He attempted to tighten his fingers around hers but could not. "I cannot strengthen my grip."

She, too, had noticed this but prayed it would be a temporary issue. "We must put our trust in God. He has spared your life."

He gave her a half smile. "Indeed, but perhaps this makes things more difficult for you."

"You are indeed surly and ungrateful tonight! I don't care if you are ailing, Ronan, you must not speak ill of God."

His dark beard had grown thicker and his hair was unruly on the feather pillow she had brought him. In such a state, he appeared strangely powerless, but she knew it was an illusion. Her father's best man would still rise and fight, should he have to. She checked a motherly urge to smooth his hair from his forehead.

He dropped his other hand over hers, taking her by surprise. His warm eyes glimmered in the lamplight, revealing an unfettered ardor. "Britta. Perhaps you know...surely you have realized that I have loved you for many years now?"

How should she respond? Her hand grew warm under his. Speaking the truth would not be easy, but she owed that to him.

"Ronan, it is true I care for you, most wholeheartedly. You are as much a part of me as our castle itself." She bowed her head. "But I cannot return that kind of love. I love you as a brother, Ronan. As a friend."

She waited a moment then untucked her chin and let her eyes meet his. He looked as if she had just kicked him, but his words were charged with tenderness and wonder.

"You love the Viking."

She nodded.

"And he loves you."

She responded quickly. "I am unsure."

He pulled her in with his eyes, and his grip tightened in urgency. "I must speak with him."

"Oh, no, I don't—"

"I will speak with him, now." Ronan's voice was firm. "Who can say if I will survive this wound?"

He was teasing her now, but she didn't like to think of Ronan's death. Embarrassing tears filled her eyes.

He placed his strong right hand on her cheek. "How I have longed to wipe your tears away, to kiss the pink of your cheeks. So many times I held back from embracing you, because your father's wishes weighed heavily on me. But it does not fall to me to do such things; I see that now. God has placed me in your life as a protector and friend, but not as a husband."

She burst into tears, and Ronan sat up and kissed her forehead.

"Now go, sweet child. Send the Viking to me."

Unable to speak or to decline his command, she left the room.

Sigfrid and his men were in fine form, sharing stories of their victory over the candlelit long table. One man claimed he killed two men with one arrow. One said Odin had smiled upon them from the raven-shaped mountain nearby. Ari leaned back in his chair, closing his eyes. The rush of urgency that had driven him in battle had dissipated, leaving him exhausted.

Sigfrid gave him a nudge. "My friend, we must sail tomorrow. You know we are well into planting season and our families will be worried."

Ari nodded. "Yes, my mother will imagine the worst." She could not withstand the death of her only remaining son.

"Perhaps you have a special good-bye planned for your Irish maiden." Sigfrid smiled.

He had no plan, but he knew he should. He could not walk away from Britta without explaining what she meant to him, although he hardly understood it himself. And this was the worst time to leave—when her attentions were focused on Ronan, and when the castle might still be vulnerable to a retributive attack.

In very fact, his desire to sail seemed to have been replaced with a pressing need to spend more time with Britta. They could walk in the gardens—he could imagine tucking sprigs of lavender into her sun-warmed hair. He could hold her small hand in his own. And perhaps he could kiss those generous lips once again...

"Ari?"

Britta's voice broke into his thoughts. Her eyes were wide with anxiety. Had something happened to Ronan?

"Ronan wishes to speak with you," she continued. So the Irishman wasn't dead, but fresh apprehension stirred in Ari's heart. Perhaps Britta had told Ronan of the kiss, and he wished to issue a challenge on her behalf.

His sword lay in its sheath by the door, but his shorter seax was tucked into a leather sheath on his belt. He had retrieved it before the battle and didn't intend to give it up again.

His men's laughter died down as he approached the door to the side room. Pushing it open gently, he could see that Ronan had been transferred to a hay-stuffed cot—not to the board they had forced him to sleep on. It was fitting, of course, that they take better care of their own.

Ronan looked haggard, his face bloodless. Ari's mother would say the man needed barely cooked meat to restore the blood he had lost. He would suggest that to Florie.

The Irishman motioned him to sit close by. Ari lowered himself to a creaky stool that could barely support his weight.

"First, I want to give you thanks for joining us. You were admirable and honorable in battle."

Ari shook his head. "I am not the one to be praised. You were ready to offer your life for mine, and I am a foreigner. Why?"

Ronan's serious gaze softened in the waning lamplight. "There is no sacrifice greater than the death of Jesus Christ for my sins. It seems a small thing for me to give my life for one man, when He gave His life for all."

Ari pondered this. One sacrifice, lasting through the ages. One sacrifice that inspired others to give more of themselves, in contrast with the endless pagan sacrifices that were meant to make lives easier.

"I wish to know your Christ," Ari said.

Ronan smiled. "It is a simple thing, but following Jesus Christ will change your life. We will pray together."

Ronan prayed first, and then Ari followed the nudge of the quiet voice he had heard so often in his soul. He told the Christ of his bitterness over his brother's death and asked Him to forgive his blackened heart. He prayed he would be able to follow His leading, even in his native land. He thanked Jesus Christ for dying so he could live eternally.

When he tentatively said, "Amen," Ronan dropped his hand on Ari's shoulder. "Now we are truly brothers."

Ari choked back sudden tears as he realized God had brought him to this land for a reason. It had nothing to do with revenge and everything to do with the restoration of his soul. In the place of his lost brother, God had given him an eternal family.

Ronan gave him rueful look. "There is something else we must discuss—Britta's future. I have no claim on her, as you know. And she has no desire to marry me." He held out a hand to silence any protests from Ari. " 'Tis true. I asked her outright, and we both know she would not lie."

Ari shifted in his seat, wishing he could encourage the man who had done so much for him. Yet he could barely quell his excitement over Britta's confession.

He leaned forward, hoping to adjust the crooked legs of the stool beneath him. But a loud rip sounded as the leather seat tore in two, depositing him solidly on the cold floor. His face froze in shock and embarrassment.

Ronan's deep chuckle filled the room. "You are indeed clumsy, Viking oaf. But no matter. If you're not too injured, may I suggest you speak with the king tomorrow and ask for his daughter's hand in marriage? It is the proper course of action, and I believe you know that."

Ari sat, rubbing his seat and thighs. Visions of a future with the princess flashed into his head. Would they sail to his home? Or stay in her castle?

Did it matter?

"Thank you for your wisdom, brother, and for sacrificing the woman you have loved. I can never repay you." He pulled himself up to a standing position, rubbing his hip.

"You can repay me by choosing sturdier chairs, Viking," Ronan said. His good-natured laughter followed Ari out the door.

CHAPTER 18

Sigfrid was alone in the great hall when Ari emerged. He jerked his thumb toward Valgerd, who lay on a makeshift cot that had been shoved into the kitchen doorway.

"He wants to be nearby, should the warrior have pains in the night," Sigfrid explained. "I will return to our camp soon." He paused, shooting Ari a knowing look. "The Irishman has given you something to think about?"

Ari nodded. "I must decide my course. Before we even sailed, you sensed that revenge was not the only thing that drove me to this land. I could not give it words, but restlessness jabbed like a dagger point into my soul. Yet now I feel a peace I could not lay hold of in our land."

"The princess?" Sigfrid guessed.

"It is true she has comforted me, but my peace comes from elsewhere. I have believed in the Christian God, Sigfrid. This is not the news my parents wanted to hear."

Sigfrid narrowed his gaze and muttered, "Perhaps you are wrong."

"What did you say?"

"Do you know your parents so little?" His old friend clasped his arm. "From the time your brother died, your parents have searched for meaning, for answers. Our gods offer them nothing. Just before you sailed, your father told me they were visiting the Christian church. They did not want you to know, for fear you would accuse them of foolishness in their old age."

His head swam. His parents? Visiting a church? He could not hide his awe. "This God is surely great, if He reaches into hearts in our land also."

Sigfrid did not agree, but he did not contradict him. "You will stay behind when we sail tomorrow?"

Ari hesitated.

Sigfrid filled in the words. "I have loved only once in my long life. You know my wife died too young. But I see in your eyes the same feeling I had for her, the same desire to protect her from the evils we have seen in the face of battle. This princess will be your first concern now—even above your parents. I will tell them of your decision to stay with her and to follow the Christian God."

He clasped Sigfrid in a hug, tears filling his eyes. "May we meet again."

"Surely we shall." Sigfrid unlatched a small pouch on his belt and handed it to him. "Here is something from home to remember us by."

Ari loosened the leather straps, and a piece of ivory walrus tusk rolled into his hand.

"Many thanks, my friend. I will treasure this as I do my bronze bottle."

Sigfrid smiled. "But soon you will have a wife to treasure more."

✦

BRITTA SAT CURLED on her bed, bare feet tucked up under her sleeping gown. Half-open books lay strewn about her like an abandoned fairy circle. She could not read more than one page tonight, it seemed. Her mind kept returning to her impossible situation.

Ari would sail tomorrow with his men. She would have to say good-bye.

Unless she stowed away with him…but no princess in her right mind would join a crew of Vikings just to be near one man who hadn't even declared his love for her yet. Besides, he was a pagan and not her husband. He would probably sell her into slavery or something equally barbaric.

She would stay home. Perhaps she would marry Ronan after all. She would be safe.

Yet in the Bible stories, God seemed to put a higher value on obedience and trust than on safety.

She prayed aloud. "Oh, heavenly Father, I do not know what You would have me do! I am so confused about Ari—the man is not a Christian, yet he pulls at my heart. You know my obligations here, that I cannot leave my father and our castle. Please point the way in the direction I must go. Close any doors I should not walk through."

Someone had stoked her fire, and her room was uncommonly cozy. She did not even pull the curtains on her bed but snuggled beneath the covers into her down mattress. Cricket chirps and night-bird warbles soothed her senses. Her thoughts ceased their tumbling and her limbs released the tension of the long day. She drifted into much-needed sleep.

◈

A DEEP, guttural scream woke Britta. Disoriented, it took her a moment to ascertain that she was still on her bed. Though a tiny flame still flickered in the hearth, the room was cloaked in darkness.

She held her breath, waiting to see where the cry had come from. It only took a moment for a terrifying sound to rend the air: her father, calling for help.

Jumping from her bed, she grabbed a candle and shoved it into the low flame of the hearth to light it. Holding it close to her chest to protect the stuttering wick, she crept from her door and stood in the hallway. Two men raced toward her father's room—she couldn't be sure in the dark, but she thought one was Ronan.

Entering the king's chamber, Britta tried to make sense of what she saw. A dark pool of blood spread under a man in a leather vest who lay facedown on the stone floor. The red-blond hair told her it was not her father who had been killed.

For the man was surely dead. A sword protruded from his back. Even as Ronan and a guard felt for his pulse, it was obvious he had not survived the blow.

She looked at the sword closely. The beautiful shine on the blade and the elongated, ornately carved hilt forced her to a horrifying realization.

It was Ari's sword.

As her father came to her side, she stepped into the comfort of his open arms. "What happened? Were you hurt?"

He squeezed her more tightly, as if he could protect her from the gruesome sight in front of them. "I was preparing for bed, and Clancy stopped in to give a report. He was going home for the night, and Garth was going to take his post and patrol this floor. I had asked them to stay tonight, in case any intruders were around."

Father didn't clarify, but she strongly suspected he counted the Viking warriors as intruders. Now it seemed his hesitation to trust them had not been unfounded.

He continued. "After Clancy put out the lamps, another

knock sounded. He went to open the door, expecting Garth. I could not see who stood there, because my fire was low. But as Clancy turned to tell me something, he must have been stabbed in the back. He fell just as he is there. When he groaned, I shouted and lit a lamp. The scoundrel fled, leaving the sword."

She could not hold back her tears. Clancy had a wife and small children. Was it possible Ari would have committed such a ruthless murder?

Her father glanced again at the incriminating sword. His voice was both reflective and foreboding. "My deepest fear about the Viking has been realized. We never convinced him that we did not kill his brother. Yet I foolishly assumed his eagerness to fight on our behalf was proof of his loyalty. Instead, it was merely a means of winning our trust and infiltrating our castle."

She wanted to protest. But her father was so widely traveled, and he had met warriors of every stripe—both friend and foe. Although she wanted to, she could not deny that his conclusions were consistent with Ari's actions.

Father's words hit her heart like flaming arrows. "Indeed, I doubt his men ever sailed. They simply waited to swoop in as our saviors, all the while plotting our demise."

She clung to his arm, all the goodness slipping out of her sheltered world. Was it true? That sunlit kiss, those caring words? The invincible way she had felt with her hand tucked into Ari's?

She tried to catch Ronan's eye, but he was busy wrapping Clancy's large body in a blanket. The sword had been removed from the man's back, but she could not bring herself to look at it again.

A guard strode in and whispered in the king's ear. Her father nodded.

"The castle has been searched, and he is not here." He spoke loudly so the others could hear. "I doubt they will attack in the night, when they are spent from the battle. Tonight we will throw their sleeping Viking healer in a cell and set a guard on the castle. At first light, as soon as my troops can prepare, we will storm the Viking camp and take no prisoners."

Ronan simply nodded, shock etching his face. He would have to deliver Clancy's body to his wife tonight. She remembered Clancy's wife—a petite brunette with wide-set doe eyes. Innocent. Oblivious.

Just as she herself had been, until Ari's sword had ripped a hole in her heart.

CHAPTER 19

Pale sunlight roused Britta from a mere hour's sleep, and she stumbled downstairs. She did not see Valgerd's cot, a sure indication he had been secured in a basement cell.

She peered into the scullery and found Florie pouring hot water into ceramic mugs. The nursemaid came to her side and hugged her gently. She motioned to the table, handing Britta a full mug of the fragrant liquid. "Please drink some, m'lady. This brew of lemon balm, lavender, and chamomile might ease your worries some."

Britta knew nothing could ease her worries, but she sat and sipped at it anyway, in hopes it would excuse her from eating. She could not eat until she knew the truth about Ari.

Father joined her at the table, wearing his tunic that would soon be covered with a mail shirt. Although she should not question her father's wisdom in kingdom matters, she had to ask one question. "Will you kill him, Father? After all he has done for us?"

He gave her a grim smile. "You have been strong, my daughter —like your mother. I regret you had to see what happened last night. But perhaps it was for the best. He had convinced us all of his goodwill—even Ronan, and that is no easy task."

Perhaps Father was right, and vengeance had driven Ari to contrive such an elaborate deception. Yet if his goal was to destroy their kingdom, surely he would not have hindered the Norman rider from capturing her yesterday?

She leaned forward, anxious to resolve the issue in her mind. "Father, where are we holding the Norman rider? Was he badly injured from his fall?"

Her father's soft gray eyes widened. "What Norman rider?"

She gasped. As soon as she had entered the castle yesterday, she had been consumed with Ronan's recovery. She had forgotten the Norman lashed to the tree, and perhaps Ari had, too.

"A Norman rider tried to charge and kill me yesterday. Ari—"

Ronan walked out of the small room, circles under his eyes. His limbs moved stiffly.

Meeting her concerned gaze, he said, "Do continue, Britta. What did you say about Ari?"

She sank deeper into her chair, sensing the disappointment in his tone. Hadn't he warned her about Ari from the start? And she had refused his advances for those of a murderous barbarian.

Guilt ridden at her own gullibility, she tried to redirect the conversation. "I am sorry you had such a sad task last night. I pray Clancy's widow finds comfort. Perhaps you should rest today, until your wound is fully healed."

Ronan shook his head, returning to the topic at hand. "You had something to share about Ari."

Before she could respond, an armed guard burst into the great hall, his sword tip pointed into the back of the very man they spoke of.

"Walked up to the castle gate, bold as bold. Asked to see you, King O'Shea."

Ari could not understand why the guard had such an arrogant tone. Hadn't he fought alongside him just yesterday? He turned to see if the man was in jest, but the sword tip pinched through his tunic into his skin, assuring him the man was in earnest.

"One more word from you, and I'll stab you in the back, just as you did our man."

Stabbed in the back? Who had been stabbed? Desperate for answers, he locked eyes with Britta. She looked tired and confused. Ronan's gaze was serious, his hand resting on his sword hilt.

King O'Shea stepped closer. "You have nothing to say, Viking?"

"Why should I say something? What has happened?"

The king's lips tightened. "Your feigned ignorance will no longer sway me." He nodded at the guard. "Take him to the cell. He can join his friend."

Friend? Who was he referring to?

The guard shoved him none too carefully to the basement door, then down the musty stone stairs. A torch on the wall hissed as it burned down, its light nearly extinguished. Valgerd's familiar voice greeted him.

"Welcome, m'lord."

They had taken the Viking healer hostage? But the man had saved Ronan's life.

Everything was upside down, the complete opposite of what it should be. The Irishmen should be praising Ari and his men, not throwing them behind iron bars.

When the door locked behind him, Ari clung to his only

hope—the God he had so recently believed in. He fell on his knees and begged Him for mercy.

◆

As soon as Ari was taken away, Father retired to his chamber to pray. Britta knew he had to act quickly or risk losing his advantage over the Vikings.

Ronan rubbed at his beard, meeting her eyes. "I am unsure."

She felt the same way, but she needed to make sense of the facts. "Ronan, we cannot explain his sword. None of our men would have killed Clancy simply to lay blame on a Viking. What Father said rings true—Ari won our trust so he could get close, and then he attempted to kill our king. We were blind and foolish."

"Yet you had come to love him," Ronan said simply.

"Yes, but perhaps my feelings led me astray—although I cannot understand why he didn't leave me to that Norman, if he wanted our castle."

"What Norman?"

"I could not elaborate earlier, but there was a straggler Norman horseman who charged us in the field. Ari thwarted him, and the man fell over a small precipice. We left him tied to a tree but forgot to retrieve him last night in my haste to come to your aid." She frowned. "I suppose the Norman's attack was fortuitous for Ari, because he protected me, making me trust him more."

"No one has checked to see if he is still there today?"

"I suppose not. After Clancy's murder—"

Ronan jumped to his feet. "Tell your father he cannot attack until I return. Then you must go and speak to Ari."

"But I—"

Ronan strode forward, cutting off her protests by gently

taking her chin in his hand and forcing her to meet his brilliant gaze.

"You will never rest if we slaughter innocent men. Yes, *innocent*. Something was not right about that sword, Britta. I have looked cold-blooded murderers in the eye, and Ari is not one of them. You know I would never put you in harm's way. I am asking you to speak to the man and find out what he has to say in his own defense."

She did not want to ask Ari for his explanation of last night —hadn't she played the fool for the man too many times already? But the fervor in Ronan's voice forced her to capitulate.

"I will do so." She determined to be wise as a serpent when she questioned the beguiling Northman. "Just be careful with your wound, whatever you do. It needs time to heal completely."

He kissed her cheek. "Of course." His dark eyes probed hers. "And you must be careful with your heart. Real love is not so easily tossed aside."

CHAPTER 20

Ari sat on the cold stone bench, wishing Valgerd could recount what the Irish guards had said when they took him away. But his friend understood little of their language and was just as perplexed as he was.

His guard had mentioned that one of their men was stabbed in the back. It seemed they had concluded it was his doing, but why?

Unless...

He sat bolt upright. He had left his sword behind when he walked Sigfrid back to camp. He had only planned to stay a short time, to speak with the men before they sailed. Yet he was so bone weary at the end of a battle day, he had drifted to sleep by the warm fire. When the sun rose, he'd woken on the dewy grass, a wool blanket draped over him. He had come straight back to the castle.

There was only one conclusion: in the meantime, someone had used his sword to murder an Irishman.

He rubbed his hand across his forehead, abhorring the filthy state he was in. He had not washed himself since the battle, so his clothing and his body were still splattered with blood and dirt.

Would he be executed in such a state? He could not let his thoughts wander that direction, yet he knew it was unlikely the king would spare his life a second time.

Valgerd had fallen silent, his light brows knit in fury. Suddenly, he grunted and leaned forward on his bench. "We never should have trusted the Irish—slippery demons. We offered up our lives for theirs in battle, and what thanks did we receive? Gold? Jewels? No. They threw us in prison. And what evil have they planned for our crew, Ari?"

Ari's empty stomach clenched. It was a valid fear. If the Irish had been so bold as to capture him, knowing he was the Viking leader, what would they do to his men? Although his crew kept weapons on their belts nearly all the time, they were relaxed and not expecting any trouble. Would Sigfrid see the Irish approaching in time to prepare for another battle?

In desperation, he loosened his belt and wrapped it around the iron bar. Perhaps he could pull the door down. He yanked it backward with all his might, but it only gave a slight creak and remained fast.

Light cut into the dark dungeon, and a rust-colored skirt dusted the steps above. When Britta's pale face came into view, he wrapped the belt around one hand, shoving it behind his back.

"Britta, I am sorry for your man's death. I know nothing about it."

She held up a slim, small hand. Her slightly imperious gaze indicated that she had come in her capacity as princess, not out of love for him.

"Ronan is not convinced that you killed Clancy." Her tone remained aloof and impersonal. "But I am not certain what to believe. Your sword was in his back."

So it was Clancy who died. He shook his head in disbelief.

First he had accidentally broken the poor man's arm, and now he could only assume his sword—his Peacebreaker—had taken the Irish warrior's life. Even more distressing, the man had been stabbed in the back, an action beneath contempt.

"I would never—"

"But someone did. And it makes sense it would have been you."

"How does that make sense? Why would I want to kill Clancy?"

"You thought he was my *father*." Her voice wavered, exposing the depth of her emotion. "You wanted the king dead so you could take our castle for your Vikings. It was your plan all along."

Did she truly believe these lies? If so, the past weeks had meant nothing to her. Yet those weeks had changed his life.

He recalled the sweetness of her lips as they had met his, the womanly feel of her waist under his palm, and how her heavy hair brushed against his hand. When he was injured, she had been so patient as she read to him, pointing out the Latin words so he could sound them out. Had it all been a ruse, a plan to win his trust before concocting an excuse to kill him?

Helplessly, he met her eyes, and he recognized an anguish that belied her harsh words. At some point, she had trusted him —perhaps even loved him?—enough to allow him to hurt her. Of course she was angered that someone had attempted to kill her father. He would try a different approach.

He pressed his face to the cold bars. "No Viking would ever leave his most treasured sword in a dead body. Ask anyone. Ask Ronan! If I wanted to slay your father—which I would never do —I would have been sure to stab the right man. And I would *not* have stabbed him in the back. I would have made him look into my eyes, even as he died. I would have been prepared to die an honorable death if captured. You know that what I am saying is true."

She stepped closer, her face pensive.

He spoke again before she could respond. "I am a Christian now, Britta. I would not kill a man in that way—like a coward."

A small gasp escaped her lips. "You are a Christian? But you never told me."

"You had already retired when I left Ronan's room." He grimaced, recalling how impatient he had been to speak with the king about marriage today. What a fool he had been, to believe a Viking would ever be accepted in this land!

As her gaze wavered between him and Valgerd, Ari spoke again. "Execute me if you deem it right, but do not attack my men. Allow them to sail home as planned."

"It is too late." Her face blanched. "My father already prepares for battle, and his men have gathered. When Ronan returns, they will attack the camp."

He gritted his teeth. Perhaps he would not be able to escape death in Ireland, but he must escape to fight with his men one last time.

"Lean in," he whispered.

She shot him a questioning look.

"Lean in toward this bar. I will not harm you, but I must go to my men and warn them. Do you believe what I have told you? That I am innocent?"

The confusion on her face melted into a slow certainty. "You have convinced me, despite my misgivings. Ronan was right to send me to speak to you. Now I realize you would never stab a man in the back, nor plot evil against my father."

She glanced at Valgerd, who stood by mutely, waiting to see what would happen. When her eyes slid back to Ari, her gaze was so intense, so searching, he had to say the words burning like hot coals inside him.

"I love you, Britta. You make my heart glad. I cannot leave this land without you."

All her hesitation seemed to give way, and she leaned into

the bar, her cold nose nearly touching his. Holding her steady gaze, he took his belt in both hands and wrapped it loosely around her neck.

"Guard!" he shouted into the darkness. "Release me or I will strangle your princess!"

◆

HEAVY STEPS POUNDED down the stairs in response to his threat. He held his ground, hoping this deception would enable his release. He tightened the belt slightly to make it more convincing, and Britta let out a sharp cry. Immediately, he loosened it, but she winked, letting him know that she, too, could play her part.

Ronan strode into the dungeon, torch aloft. He had tucked his mace into his belt. His dark gaze was hard to interpret.

"Drop the belt, Ari. I know what has happened, and I have told the king."

What did this mean? Ari kept the leather strap taut. "I will not. You must explain."

Ronan walked up to the cell, inserting a key in the lock, which forced Ari to drop the belt before the door swung open.

Britta did not hesitate but rushed into the small space to stand by Ari. Ronan did not restrain her. That could only mean one thing.

The Irish warrior believed him. Relief and thankfulness flooded Ari. He boldly slipped an arm around Britta, and she sank into his side. But urgency to save his men propelled him to speak again.

"What did you tell the king? Will your men attack? I must know."

Ronan's smile unknotted the fears that had held him hostage. "I told the king to stay his attack on your Vikings. You did not murder Clancy. It was the Norman."

"The Norman!" His eyes dropped under Ronan's steady gaze. Of course. He had been so enthralled by Britta's kiss, then so distracted by her single-minded concern for Ronan, he had forgotten to send someone for the wounded Norman. He had eaten and slept and forgotten his captive strapped to a tree. It was shameful.

Ronan continued. "The man somehow loosened his binds and escaped, but he still craved a Norman victory. He crept into the castle through the gardens and took up your sword—"

"Peacebreaker." Ari strengthened his grip on Britta's waist, wishing he could distract her from the recitation of his failures. "I realized I had left it behind when I reached our camp, but I fell asleep before I could return for it."

As if sensing Ari's discomfort, Ronan hastened to tell the rest of the story. "The man did not take long to locate the king's chamber, and he decided to steal in and murder him. When Clancy opened the door, the Norman assumed the man was our king and took the opportunity to stab him when he turned. But when he heard the king's shout and realized others were coming, he tore down the back staircase."

Ari groaned. "He knew the sword would point to a Viking attack."

"Of course. Even though his plan to kill the king failed, it could still be effective if we rose up against your Vikings. Then the Normans could return and take the castle in the midst of the chaos."

Choking back his own guilt, Ari spoke. "And now a man lies dead because of my grievous mistakes. How many others could have died because of them?"

Britta did not respond with anger toward him, but toward the murderous Norman. "Where has this conniving Norman run off to, Ronan?"

Ronan put an arm on hers. "Steady. He was caught in the next town, raiding eggs from a henhouse. The farmer sent word to the castle that he had a Norman prisoner. Once I knew the man was alive, it was easy to ascertain the true events of last night."

Valgerd rapped at the bars, impatient with their discussion. He used one of the few Irish words he knew. "Freedom!"

"You will have it." Ronan calmly unlocked the other cell door. He motioned to Valgerd. "Now go, and report to your men that all is well with your leader."

Valgerd waited as Ari translated, adding his own instructions. "Tell them I am safe, and that they must sail while the wind is good." He allowed his gaze to drop to Britta's luminous, undoubting face. "And tell them I will not be sailing with them."

CHAPTER 21

Clinging to Ari's hand, Britta followed Ronan up the stairs into the great hall. Father and his men sat at the table. The warriors had removed their chain mail and spoke easily as Florie set food before them.

"See if that won't hearten the lot of you," Florie said. When she saw Britta, she winked. "It's been altogether tense without you around, m'lady. I take it Ronan has explained things to you?"

Britta nodded. Father summoned her closer, and she released Ari's hand to draw near to his side. His eyes were filled with regret.

"I have wronged you, Britta—and our kingdom. I made bad assumptions and nearly launched into a war with innocent men. We would have been no better than the Normans who attacked us without cause. Will you ever be able to forgive me?"

"Of course I forgive you, Father. But there is someone else we have both wronged." She looked at Ari.

The king stood and faced the Viking. Ari hunched down a bit, as if he wished to disappear from the eyes of the Irish warriors who had so quickly turned against him.

"Ari Thorvardsson," Father began.

Britta nudged his elbow. "It is Thor*vald*sson, Father."

"Yes. Well, it is best I learn to say your name properly, Ari Thorvaldsson. You have given much for my kingdom, and I have yet to repay you. I understand today is the day you set sail. Before you do, I would like to offer you your choice of treasure from my coffers. I will lead you to them myself."

Ari straightened. His appearance grew more imposing, even with his unkempt hair and clothing. Britta wondered again if his family was in a high position in his country, because his bearing did seem regal.

"There is only one thing I ask," Ari said.

Florie beamed at Britta from across the room, her cheeks rounded in a wide smile. Ronan was focused on the Viking, his lips in a resigned line.

Britta started, realizing what Ari might request. Her hands went numb, and she sat down abruptly to forestall a swoon. If he asked to marry her, her father might still refuse. Yet if he requested some other treasure, her heart might break forever.

"I would ask to be your bondservant for a half year," Ari finished.

Father's carefully positioned smile faded. "But why?"

A hush fell over the room as Ari explained. "Because, King O'Shea, I love your daughter. Yet our days together have ended in turbulence. This is no way to start a marriage. Instead, if I stay and serve you, I can prove my loyalty." He bowed his head in respect. "I also wish to aid Clancy's widow and family, to make amends for my careless behavior."

Blood rushed back into her hands. She rose to her feet and faced the king. "Oh, Father, please allow it! He is an honest man. I never should have doubted him. And now he has become a Christian man as well."

Her father's eyebrows shot up. "Is this true?"

Ronan stepped forward to answer. "Yes, I know it is." He

paused, thoughtful. "And if we let him stay, he will become more grounded in the faith, because Britta could read the Bible to him. Perhaps he could share more about Christianity with his people, who have already begun to convert."

She gave Ronan a thankful look then clasped her father's hand as if she were a small child begging for a gift. "Please."

Father looked from her to Ronan to Ari. His men looked on, awaiting his decision. Florie wrung her hands on her apron.

Finally, he spoke. "I offered you a reward, and although you did not ask for any of my goods, I see you have a greater treasure in mind. As my daughter said, you are an honorable man. I grant your request. You have safe haven in my kingdom as long as you choose to stay. But do not stay as a bondservant. I ask you to stay as our friend."

Britta's tears mingled with laughter as she moved to stand by Ari.

He took her hand in his then responded to her father. "I will stay of my own accord, but I promise I will be here a half year." He leaned down to her ear, his low, determined voice setting her heart racing. "I promise," he repeated.

"It is settled," Father said. "Now please, go and bid your men farewell so they may sail in peace. When you return, we must determine where you will live. There is room in the castle, of course, but it might not be circumspect, given your feelings for my daughter."

Florie burst out, "He's welcome to stay with us, m'lord. Clancy's widow and bairns live near our abode, and if he wishes to work for his supper, my James could use an extra hand on the farm."

Ari smiled. "I would welcome the work."

Britta squeezed his hand, unable to contain her joy. Ari was willing to leave his family and friends behind, to learn more about her God, her people, and *her*.

How had her love so easily faded to distrust? Ronan was

right—real love was not so easily tossed aside. Trust was based on a person's character, who you knew them to be. Ronan had guessed that Ari was incapable of such a cowardly murder. Yet she had let fear drive her suspicions, overlooking the honorable way Ari had always behaved.

As Father and his men dug into their meal, Ari led Britta outside and through the castle gate. The fallen soldiers had been removed, so only bloodstains and torn turf remained to show what a vicious battle it had been. The crisp air and snow-white clouds gave her the feeling that God was trying to sweep the land of its sadness.

Ari stopped abruptly, angling her to face him. He located her wrists under her voluminous sleeves. Circling them in his fingers, he gently traced her arms up to her elbows. The sweetness of his touch contrasted with the strength of those hands—hands that had wielded swords and steered ships.

"Remember what you promised," he said. "You will teach me to read if I teach you my language. I want you to understand every word I say, Britta."

It would never become tiring, to hear her name on his lips. She looked into the limitless blue of his eyes, so like the ocean. His blond lashes caught the sunlight.

"And I want you to understand this," she said, wiping a smudge of battle dirt from his face. "You have showed me your valor and your honor many times, never once asking for my thanks. But I thank you, Ari Thorvaldsson. And I hope to kiss you again…once you have had a chance to wash yourself."

Laughing, she lightly pushed him forward, so he could say good-bye to his men. Would he be happy here, in her land?

Only time would tell.

CHAPTER 22

One Year Later, Summer

Dangling her bare feet in the creek, Britta knew her hemline would be drenched, but she did not care.

She munched an apple, puckering her mouth at its tartness. Florie would tell her that eating too many early apples would upset her stomach and ruin her meal, but she felt like fully indulging today.

After all, there was much to celebrate.

The Normans had agreed not to invade their kingdom again, once their prisoner had been sent home, bearing gruesome tales of Viking warriors protecting the area. Her father had banded with other Irish kings and it seemed that much of Ciar's Kingdom would be saved.

Ari had stayed longer than he'd promised—a full year had passed since he had arrived on their shores. James had taken him under his wing as if he were his own son. With plenty of assistance, Ari had learned to read Latin fluently. Now he and James challenged each other to memorize scripture.

She leaned back into the moss, resting her head in her hands as she watched the thin clouds drift by. A smile broke across her face as she considered the tangible proof of Ari's love for her.

Only this morning, Ari had finished building his own home—a longhouse in Viking style. He had asked for her preferences each step of the way, from the wood they chose for the door to the perfect spots for windows. Tucked into the hillside with its turf-covered roof and wooden beams, it looked cozy and inviting, nothing like the cold castle she had grown up in.

It looked like a home, and she prayed it could be hers.

He had not asked her yet. He was determined to build his house before the leaves dropped from the trees, and she had never seen a man so single-minded. What Ari determined to do, he most certainly accomplished.

Over the past few months, she had reveled in his touches, for Ari did not withhold affection from her. Yet there were times when the clench of his fingers, the darkening of his eyes told her they were on dangerous ground. At those times, he would inevitably remember some chore he needed to do for James, and he would leave her abruptly. She knew he was trying to protect them both, and she loved him all the more for it.

Ronan still lived nearby, advising her father. But he no longer looked at her in the same way. It seemed that as his friendship with Ari had strengthened, theirs had deteriorated, yet all was as it should be. Ronan, loyal as he was to her family, would not have been the man for her. She prayed every night that God would bring him a woman to soothe his wounded heart.

"Deep in thought, I see." Ari's voice sounded behind her, and she sat up abruptly, her half-eaten apple rolling into the creek.

"Now look what you've done! That was my last apple."

He opened his palm, exposing two more of the tiny green apples. "I know how you crave these sour beauties, although I cannot understand why."

She took them and tucked them into her favorite leather

pouch. The pouch was useful when she went on walks, allowing her to gather unusual rocks, colorful feathers, or other things that caught her eye.

She noted Ari's bronze bottle dangling from a cord on his belt. "Why did you bring your bottle? Are you so very thirsty? This creek is full of fish."

He unlatched the bottle, and she noticed its gleam. He must have polished it recently. When he handed it to her, she touched the dent the mace had left.

"How different our lives could have been," she said, tears springing to her eyes. "What if Florie's aim had been true?"

"But it was not, for God willed otherwise." He shot her a curious look, as if waiting for her to notice something.

She turned the bottle over in her hands, examining it. "It looks beautiful, so shiny." Something rattled inside. "What is this?"

He took the lid from the top. "You won't know unless you look."

She peered into the darkness then tilted it toward the sunlight. A pale object clattered about then slid from the bottle's neck into her hand.

"Oh!" She managed to catch it before it fell to the ground. Looking at it closely, she realized it was an ornately carved piece of ivory. The ivory itself was slightly marbled, but the beauty was in the designs. She could make out a longship and a castle, as well as Crow Mountain. And in the middle were a couple—a warrior and a maiden—and the word *Spero* wreathed around their heads.

"Hope," she breathed.

"I carved this for you," he said simply.

"I know," she said.

He cleared his throat. "There is always hope. This bottle bears that word upon its rim, but the poor Irish monk who owned it probably died in one of our raids."

She nodded, unable to speak.

"Yet here we stand—a Viking warrior and an Irish princess—both hoping in the same God the monk believed in. Perhaps he is smiling on us from heaven."

She swallowed, touching the polished ivory. "How much thought you have put into this!"

"I have thought of little else. I wanted to give you a gift that was a piece of myself—my home—and that is what this walrus ivory is. I do not paint, but I thought you would like a carving of us."

"Thank you," she said, looking closer at the grooved pictures. "But what are these figures here behind me? They look as if they are tearing at my skirt! Are they wild dogs?"

He burst into laughter. "No, those are your children, clinging to your skirts."

"My children?"

"Our children." His smile faded into a look of earnestness that tore at her already surrendered heart. He touched her cheekbone, letting his fingers trail down to her chin. "I love you, Britta. You must know I built the house for you—for us. Your father knows of my plans, and he has given me his blessing. Will you be my wife?"

Throwing herself into his strong arms, she nodded. "Yes, yes! Please be my husband!"

He whirled her around, even as she clutched the ivory in one hand, the bottle in the other. When he set her down, she nearly toppled into the creek in her dizziness, but he pulled her close and pressed a tender kiss on her lips. She could not wait to kiss him more, anytime she wished.

"We will marry tomorrow," he said decisively.

She did not think twice. "Of course we will."

HER FATHER CAME to her as Florie buttoned her wedding gown, which was nearly the same color as the ivory tusk. It was her mother's dress, and it fit perfectly.

He sighed. "You will stay nearby, in the longhouse? I would not like to have you far from me."

"Of course we will stay close. And now Ronan can live in the castle, where he can learn your ways and prepare to rule someday."

Father frowned. "Why would he want to rule?"

She turned, and a peach rose that Florie had twined in her hair fell to the floor. The nursemaid huffed amiably and searched for another one to replace it.

"Why, because Ronan will inherit the kingdom, of course. If he moved in, it would make things so much easier."

"Ronan is not to inherit my kingdom, Britta. *You* are. You are my child, my own blood, so you must take over for me. Unless you do not wish to do so?"

She grasped his hands, her knuckles turning white. All these years, she had been certain the castle and the kingdom would go to Ronan because her father had no male heir. But he had always planned to give it to her. She could stay in the land she loved, help the people she loved, for the rest of her life.

"But what of Ari? He will be my husband."

"It is your decision. If you want him to rule alongside you, so he shall. If you want to be queen, you may rule by yourself."

She did not need to ponder. "If I am queen, he must be king and command equal respect, even without the O'Shea name."

"It will be as you say, my dearest. Now I will go and let Florie arrange your hair, and doubtless weep a little, too."

She hugged him. "Thank you, Father, for understanding my heart."

"It is a queen's heart." He kissed her forehead before he strode out.

As Father had anticipated, Florie immediately burst into

tears. When her sobs slowed, she said, "My little book-loving girl to be queen! Imagine!"

Britta glanced out the window, catching sight of Ari in his white tunic threaded with gold. She smiled. God had answered her prayers in a way she had never imagined—bringing peace and hope to her kingdom on the distant tide.

MORE BOOKS BY HEATHER DAY GILBERT

Looking for more Vikings?

Be sure to check out Heather Day Gilbert's *Vikings of the New World Saga* at **heatherdaygilbert.com** — a 2-book series based on the real Viking women who sailed to North America.

And if you're anxious to read Hearts of Ireland Book 2, *The Secret Haven*, which will feature Ronan's story, please be sure to sign up for Heather's newsletter at heatherdaygilbert.com for announcements as to its publication date.

If you enjoyed *The Distant Tide*, please be sure to leave an online review and share about it with your friends! Thank you!

Made in the USA
Las Vegas, NV
03 November 2021